TWENTY-THREE 03

A NEW GENERATION

MARQUS CREAVALLE

CONTENTS

FINAL BRIEFING

"*E*veryone please take your seats."

The two dozen men and women in identical one-piece black bodysuits settled into their chairs. The room was large, perfectly circular, and everything about it was meant to impart equality. From the twin rings of tables with chairs that floated out from beneath on a cushion of magnetically charged air, to the soft lighting that emanated from the walls and floors and ceiling, the briefing room for the Protectorate's Romanian branch of academy cadets was one of rounded edges and clear sightlines.

Two rows of wraparound tables and their legless chairs followed the curving walls to look down on a four-foot-wide white circular disk set into the floor. Captain Nest, their tough but feminine head instructor, cast her gaze up at the two levels as the men and women followed her command to sit. She was tall and slender, with the strength and weight of a ballerina. But her musculature was augmented by cybernetics to the degree she could crush a much larger man's hand by shaking it, a move she had done more than once to put a beefy cadet in his place.

She squinted slightly to zoom in on the faces and hands of her students. Her implanted lenses did this for her easily, and she noted some bore healing wounds, yet none showed evidence of the obvious discomfort the slashed and heavy blows had initially caused and continued to provide. She said nothing to this but internally felt pride at the group of early 20-somethings whom she had beaten, guided, challenged, and molded not wanting to show weakness before her.

An older man stepped into the room and came to stand beside her. He wore a white lab coat that touched his knees, had the soft, slouching step of the lifelong academic, and he carried a clear plastic rectangle. She nodded at him and he returned the gesture, reaching up to scratch his week's worth of gray stubble. He stood off to one side as she closed her eyes and tapped the lids twice.

"March 25th, 2303. 0745 hours. In a moment, we will review the runs you all completed two days prior," she said as she opened her eyes and held out her hands. Through the lenses she wore, a grid pattern of glowing lines, words, and images appeared, and she typed and swiped portions of the holographic screen she alone could see as she talked to the others. "The positive aspects, and those which require correction."

A group of women seated on one end of the top ring grinned and gave each other looks. "And then we'll get to the good part, right, Captain?"

Captain Nest turned to look up at the woman. The trainee was 21, slim and hard of muscle and wore her sandy blonde hair pulled back in cornrows. She sat in the chair with her legs splayed out and her shoulders cocked at an angle. It was the posture of a woman certain of her place in the coming structure of operators, and with no doubt, she would leave the Cicada Program's cadet class to arrive at Agent in short order. Nest did not return the woman's smile.

"If you're referring to the final stage of your candidacy, then yes. We will cover it. But not before we address the successful aspects of the missions you all most recently went on. Paying particular attention to the parts where you dropped the ball."

The young woman grinned and leaned back with crossed arms, clearly not cowed by the tone of her leader. Others in the room showed the same bravado, but not all. Several looked troubled, and more than one was stone-faced.

"We will touch on the overall assignments of each team, prior to introducing the Final Exam," Nest said, waving her hands and causing the round white disk in the floor to glow, "but I want to put special focus on one. That of Aveen's team."

A group of four sitting on the lower ring nearer to the brightening disk looked up. Each of them wore wounds closed by the nanite gel applied in the field from their medical kits, and more than one showed faint burns on their hands. Aveen, a square-jawed 23-year-old, sat up a little straighter as his team was singled out. He showed neither fear nor concern at the attention, and this posture was mirrored by his second-in-command, Celeste. The younger members of his team, Benji and Tofe, were another story. Benji's cheeks took on a broccoli tone at the announcement of his team being profiled, and Tofe's expression was that of one long-familiar with being blamed for mistakes. Neither showed fear, however. That had been beaten out of them from the first days in the program.

Nest considered the quartet as the room's central disk began to smoke. In actuality, the mist was a swarm of nanites that rose and assembled themselves into a 3-dimensional version of the file Nest opened. Aside from the training rooms, field courses, and PSYOPs instruction, the disk was the room's primary teaching apparatus. The records of the runs carried out by the men and women seated at the twin rings of overlooking tables were downloaded upon their return to the castle in the Romanian mountains and analyzed as much for areas of improvement for the trainees as basic intelligence-gathering for the Protectorate. This only happened when they synced their lenses to record the events of the missions, which left sections empty. These were usually the approaches and retreats from the target areas; when their targets were in sight they were ordered to record.

Nest turned her gaze to Aveen as the nanite cloud shimmered in a palate of colors and assembled into the shape of a tall building.

Promising. He will lead well. He already did in order to make it out of the conference tower.

What she actually said as she looked at the muscular dark-haired man with a serious expression locked on the solidifying cloud at the center of the room was not so complimentary. "Aveen's team faced a Level Three locked-down building in a crowded urban space and had clear instructions to eliminate the target within and to not engage with any security if at all possible. It is evident things did not go according to plan."

Celeste, a slender woman of 21 on his left, leaned toward him enough to whisper. "We got the job done. Don't blame yourself for the alarm. I scouted the run down to the last drainpipe. We didn't trip it."

He did not look at her but kept his eyes ahead, and Celeste sighed as she resumed her ramrod-straight position.

However, the woman behind them did respond.

"Checked out the drain pipes, huh? No wonder you guys fucked up. ICE's in the walls, windows, and doors. You know, *inside* the building."

Celeste turned her head barely an inch and spoke softly. "Eat a dick, Ceelon."

The woman behind her chuckled. "Seems like you got that spot covered, honey. You're the one on Team Sausage Cart. Should've been with my Valkyries, girly."

Celeste was about to fully turn back when Captain Nest cleared her throat. "You have something to add, trainee?"

Ceelon dropped the smirk, but the impression of it lingered as she looked away from her superior with a thoughtful frown. "I was just concerned that Aveen's team will have their feelings hurt from how badly they muffed their assignment. The alarm being tripped at the hotel was something a rookie would have done, not a group about to graduate. That would have gotten them a month in the cooler, but here they are. I just hope they're not here to suffer for it too much before General Aepal hands down the punishment."

Nest allowed the insinuation to settle over the room before hammering them with reality. And when it came, even Ceelon was quiet.

"They are not being sanctioned. They are being recognized for overcoming an unforeseen obstacle. And that was something they could not have predicted, nor prepared for." She looked up and met Aveen's eyes. "The alarm was set off by someone intending them to be caught. They were meant to be killed by building security, and our program's existence made public."

Silence settled onto the room as the meaning of their leader's words sank in. The threat of detection was part of the job, but in the 30 years the Protectorate's secret program of intelligence-gathering assassins had carried out missions to keep the wheels of the world turning in the post-apocalyptic reality they lived in, no leaks had occurred. It wasn't just a code of silence the members kept; any hint of someone attempting to reveal Project Cicada resulted in a swift and complete elimination of that person and anyone who they might have so much as shared a coffee with around the time the leak happened. Whole families had been wiped out, with several later being shown they could not possibly have known anything about the program. But the Protectorate erred on the side of caution. And the dead cannot talk.

The temperature of the room seemed to drop and the mood with it. Then one of the trainees spoke.

"They would have to be someone good enough to get past the building's security, and simultaneously know Aveen's team was there. They would have to know our procedures, as well as our intention of being there."

Nest looked to the man who had spoken. Huginn was a slender figure, whip-thin and wiry, and his team was known for slithering into impossible places and escaping just as remarkably.

Clever. He will be a solid strategist for us, or an attractive double agent for the enemy.

Nest made a mental note of ordering an updated morality probe for all trainees. It wasn't necessary for most of those in the room, but a man as smart as the one who had just cut through the mystery of Aveen's team's botched run would guess something was up if she required only him to take it.

"Yes," she said after a pause, "that is our finding as well. Someone with knowledge of both our program and our methods was on-site, and they tripped the alarm in the hopes of seeing Aveen's team captured or killed."

A woman on the higher level table raised a hand and Nest called for her to speak. "I don't understand. If they wanted Aveen and the others captured, why not simply tell the security forces to arrest them? Send an anonymous datalink on a one-shot, and have them just wait for the team to walk in the door?"

Nest considered the woman. It was a reasonable line of thinking, but it lacked the subtlety of the man who spoke before her. "Anything you send can be traced back. Maybe not easily, but if it arrived, it had to have left from somewhere. A one-shot has electronic components and programs that a clever datasmith can sort through and work backwards from to find the point of origin. We do it as standard procedure."

Huginn spoke again. "Meaning the only way the Skip could be sure they'd get the message across without leaving a trace, was to be present. A handheld scrambler could do it. Just figure out the alarm's signal and send an interrupt pattern, and off it pops. No fingerprints, no physical material left behind. It's what I would do."

"What makes you think it was a Skip?" the woman on the upper tier asked.

Huginn shrugged. "No one else makes sense. Like you said, they wanted the team caught or killed, and like Captain Nest pointed out, a one-shot can be traced. So it makes sense Clarion hired a merc to do it. And since we're sitting here talking about it, it worked."

Nest nodded. *Definitely need to watch him.*

"Whoever the individual was is irrelevant," she went on, moving her hands in the air to manipulate the nanite controls. "We've broken through the security codes of the building itself. By matching the frequency of them as a whole, and crossing their pathways with the thermal shifts in the rooms of the floor above the target's, below it, and the floor he was on itself, we've come up with this."

She flared her fingers and spread her arms slowly—an artist giving the nanite diorama at the center of the room instructions to swell far beyond its customary size. The building zoomed up and outward, and the three floors she indicated bloomed out to the edge of the open space bordered by the first level's ring table. This caused the nanites to lose much of their definition, and the detail of the room was greatly reduced. But it was evident a figure stood there.

"This is our suspect. We believe it is a man, based on the gait, height, and approximate proportions. But this is the best we have at the moment. Thermals cannot provide details."

All of the trainees leaned in to stare at the figure, their floating magnetic seats moving several inches in the air beneath the round tables. The silhouette was undefined, but obviously human. Not too tall, nor short. Neither fat nor thin. It was little more than a silvery cloud in human form, but it was the best they had to start with.

"We matched the time of the alarm's sounding to the energy pulse provided by this individual," Nest explained, and she held her hands like claws and rotated the room so that different angles of the figure holding something were shown to all. "The room was adjacent to the target's, the time was within two seconds of the alarm tripping, and this person left no image on any security camera. There is no doubt this is our man. Whether he was sent by Clarion is impossible to determine."

"But how are we seeing him at all?" Ceelon asked, cocking her head at the hazy figure.

"Thermals, remember?" Celeste said, giving the woman a dismissive smirk. "Captain mentioned the electrical signals flowing through the floors, and that she crossed it with the temperature fluctuations in the rooms close enough to affect the alarm. The person's body heat gave the presence, and the electricity passing through the air was broken by his body. Put them together and you've got a shadow to start playing with. You know, the stuff that flows *inside* of buildings?"

Ceelon made a suggestive back-and-forth gesture at Celeste with a semi-closed fist in her lap under the table, and Captain Nest pretended not to see it as she brought her hands back together. This compressed the building back down to a three-foot tower on the center of the disk's platform. "General Aepal was briefed on the run and determined that Aveen and his crew responded well. It is unlikely Clarion had their own personnel in the building, so as Huginn suggested a Skip is our best guess."

"Have we already interrogated the known operators?" a heavy-set man on the opposite side of the room asked.

Nest nodded. "It is happening as we speak. But you all know how difficult it is to track down the good mercs, and Clarion would only contract with a top Skip. So it is unlikely we'll find him in the next 24 hours."

"Any idea why Aveen's team was targeted?" a woman sitting at the lower table asked.

"No," Nest replied, preparing to end the discussion and move on. "Since it wasn't a direct attack on any of his team, we think it was more of a test to gauge the ability of them. If they responded well, as they did, then the message to Clarion is clear: the Protectorate is ready for you."

She used the building's thermo-electrical features to show the team carrying out its mission. They were as unsubstantial and lacking details as the Skip had been, but when the alarms began blaring on the three floors the cadets could see in the nanite cloud, the figures of the four moved with purpose and without hesitation.

"The Skip attempted to throw them off their run, but they completed their mission and evaded capture," Nest said, as the four exited the building by flying away from it on wingsuits lifted by a personalized magnetic field. "General Aepal's decree that they receive no punishment was based on them being innocent of the error after we tracked down this individual you've just met. But more importantly, because they overcame it successfully."

"In fact," she went on, swiping a hand across the tower and causing it to pulverize into a cloud of nanites that slowly drifted down into the white disk where they vacuumed into the sides, commending them on adjusting to the unexpected pressure, "the experience also led the general to the realization that someone with inside knowledge had set off the alarm."

Nest's expression grew hard. "Meaning there is a traitor in our ranks. And when we find them, a month in the cooler would be a warm oil rubdown and a margarita compared to what they will receive."

She let the threat sink in for several seconds before speaking again. "Let's move on to the final exam. Carry out the mission you're assigned, and you will graduate. Fail, and you will be removed from the program. Doctor?"

The older man who opened the debriefing with her stepped forward. Dr. Nelson was a tall and thin black man, with a shaved head and a short salt and pepper beard. His white lab coat seemed to glow in the pale light from the walls all around them, and he carried a flat piece of blank plastic. "The last assignment you will have as trainees will be a solo one. You will have full autonomy in the field, and you will have minimum gear. The test will challenge you from start to finish. And there will be a complication during the run you must adjust to."

He tapped the plastic board he carried and the central disk's nanites flowed up to take the shape of Romania mapped in 3D. "You will leave the castle tomorrow before sunset and take supersonic transport to your designated target area. Whether it is a mountain, a ballroom, a sewer, or a sandy beach, you will not know until you arrive there. You must identify your quarry, terminate him or her, and evade capture in escaping. Return here successfully and you will be promoted. Fail on any count, and you will no longer be a part of the program."

Nest stepped forward, her tone brisk. "Thank you, Doctor. Due to the nature of the exam, none of you will know who the others are targeting, nor even what part of the country they'll be in. But make no mistake, the people you will end are necessary cogs in the machinery of the rebellion."

As she spoke she let her gaze move around the room, and her eyes rested on every face for a little more than a second. It was her way of offering a piece of her attention to the collected group. It gave them the impression she was speaking to them personally, that they alone were on the receiving end of her focus.

"The targets are not as sexy as I know some of you would like. They are not rebel leaders, bounties of the Protectorate, or suicide plaguers. But these are the nuts and bolts of the terrorists. By day they are the dentists, the accountants, the veterinarians, and the shop owners of the nation. But they are also the pieces who keep the sputtering machine of the rebellion running. Remove them, and you throw a monkey wrench into the works. They are the conduits for much of the funds and supplies heading out beyond the Fence. And once you've cleared your final training assignment, we will assemble you as full agents into teams. There is even the chance you'll head into the DOX for a round of deep cleaning. That is: directly confronting Clarion."

Every floating seat shifted at this. "Are you saying we're all crossing the Fence?" Huginn asked, his expression unreadable.

Doctor Nelson cleared his throat. "We have received intelligence that the enemy is preparing to unleash a new variant of the original pathogen. Something mutated and even more virulent. Since we have seismic mines on all borders, and plasma cannons and sprayers watching the skies, the Fence is the only option. And it may not be only the Romanian Protectorate. The other provinces are potentially at risk as well."

"They can't go high, and they can't go low," Nest said, her tone serious in spite of the almost sing-song words, "so they have to go through. Your last assignment as Cicadas is to sever the waypoints Clarion depends on. If it is successful, there is a good chance the enemy will call off the assault."

Dr. Nelson reminded them the restrictions for biohazardous encounters were in full effect. "As Captain Nest noted, these are the lifelines to the resistance in the DOX. See to it that you follow protocols, so that your lives don't get snuffed out along with those of the targets. All of the targets are within our borders, so there should be no contamination from the DOX. But remember that these are the people who are helping Clarion to bring in the virus. Treat them and their surroundings accordingly."

Aveen raised his hand, speaking for the first time. "Are any targets confirmed Peds?"

Captain Nest spoke before Nelson could. "We have no intelligence to that effect. But you are to assume everyone in their vicinity is a carrier. Take your immune ramps along with performance peaks. And decontamination protocols will be waiting for you on your return. Dismissed."

The groups rose from their tables and filed out, and Nelson watched them go. Some nodded at him and others smiled, but nearly all made some acknowledgment of him as they left. He watched the quiet ones like Huginn and Aveen pass by with no comment, as well as those laughing and shoving each other with the bravado young soldiers leaned on when hiding their anxiety. He watched them leave with a sad smile and small sigh, then shook his head.

"The young never really change, do they?"

Captain Nest stood staring at the lines of reports and reconnaissance images floating in the air a few feet from her face and offered a wry sniff as she reached out and flicked aside things Nelson couldn't see. "I'd say the old have the same problem. Or maybe it's just you. What are you, 75? 80?"

He chuckled. "I'm 55, thanks. And you're 35. Too old to be a young smartass and too young to be as sentimental as you think I am."

She shrugged, whipping aside aerial surveys and sending them to their respective trainees. "You were 25 when the plague hit, so you got to live in the world before the war. I was five and don't remember much. But I'd be nostalgic too for the days I could walk down the street without worrying someone was going to jump out of the bushes and cough terminal hallucinations in my face. Yet here we are."

Nelson sighed. "Yes, here we are."

Nothing was said for half a minute, with the older man letting his mind wander to the younger days she mentioned, and hers focused on the one of their present. Finally, he nodded at her.

"I'm going to the lab to do some more work on that latest batch of divergents. There is a particularly promising animal I want to run some tests on. Let me know when the cadets return."

She grunted by way of response and he walked out, his mind split between the world of his early twenties and that of the men and women who were about to enter the dark and mutated one of their own.

AVEEN

*2*0 hours after leaving the briefing room, Aveen and his team stood at the end of the bridge that marked the edge of the compound. The training facility they had called home for the majority of their lives rose up in the gloom on the span's other side, and it was clear he was not the only one who was nervous at the coming trials. Not that it was visibly apparent. The Cicadas were the elite kill squads of the Protectorate and had long before lost the stomach-churning fear of leaving the gothic renaissance castle within the curl of Romania's western mountains.

He looked up at the façade awash in the setting sun as he always did when leaving for a mission. It had frightened him when he first saw it, as he walked alongside the junior trainee assigned to be his mentor.

~

But the older boy he was with—Glider—radiated confidence, and Aveen tried to match his firm stride and straight back as they walked over the thousand-year-old cobblestones.

"This castle was built a long time ago," Glider had said, his bright blue eyes staring up at the rising lines of heavy gray stone and points of the many small towers with their red roof work that ended in spiked needles of iron.

"It was built by a man who was fighting against invasion, just as we are. In John Hunyadi's time of the 1440s, Romania was under constant attack by the Ottoman Empire, and he did everything he could to protect this land from the men who would see it burn."

They stopped walking when they reached the other side of the bridge and Aveen tilted his head back to look up at the towers that seemed to pierce the sky. The castle was imposing; the building seemed to hunch massive shoulders downward as it considered the small boy standing before it. The sun was setting behind them and the flaming brush of it painted the millennia-old edifice with warm orange and golden color. The sun's rays made the place less forbidding, but no less intimidating.

Aveen had never heard of Hunyadi or the Ottomans. Education in the farming districts where he was settled was limited. There were many people from all over Europe who had fled to the former Romania after 70 percent of the continent fell into the hallucinatory violence or apathy of dreamscape. He wasn't sure where he was actually born, but he could work, and that was enough to earn food. He could read and write, but the only things he was ever permitted to read were the stories the Protectorate posted in the town squares where children learned of the terrible mutants and murderers that roamed beyond the magnetic fence bordering the nation. The only writing he had ever done was salutary notes praising the memory of the patriots who had died fighting the inhuman scourge on the other side of the glimmering barrier.

But Glider spoke of history—actual history—and Aveen asked him with eagerness that he couldn't hide how he had learned of the castle's story. And what other sources of the past he knew and could share.

The older boy smiled, his eyes coming down from the walls to stare at the stones in front of them. "There isn't a lot here, I'm afraid. I had to pick it up from the old folks who teach us. Dr. Nelson knows a lot, and so does Elisa."

"Who are they?"

Glider shrugged, the movement looking cool and effortless to the younger boy. "Doc Nelson is the physician for the center. He'll be the one patching you up when you break bones and slice open skin. And that'll happen a lot," he added, his smile knowing in a way that told Aveen he had visited the doctor his fair share. "But once you learn how to protect yourself, it's your classmates who will be getting the house calls. And I'll be the one making sure you learn as fast as you can."

The prospect of regular injury was hardly appealing, but Aveen was used to pain. All children of the Protectorate were. It was as common as breathing, and one couldn't hold one's breath forever. And the idea he would be learning from the older boy beside him sent a tingle of excitement coursing up his spine.

He swallowed, trying to tamp down his eagerness. "And Elisa? Who is she?"

Glider expression softened, the look becoming more thoughtful as he looked down at the edge of the bridge. "She's older than Nelson. 40, I think. And she is something of an anomaly."

Aveen blinked. "Anomaly?"

"Yeah. She's not like the others."

Aveen felt lost. "I don't understand. She's different? Like, she looks strange? Or has some special job?"

Glider chuckled, the sound dropping a swooping feeling into Aveen's stomach. "She doesn't have a third arm, if that's what you mean. But yes, she has a job not like the other people you'll work with. She's a *Mencist*."

Aveen's stomach turned again, this time unpleasantly. He had heard of these people. They were whispered of with fear and suspicion, and given all manner of powers that in centuries past would be termed witchcraft.

Glider must have seen some of the terror on his new charge's face. He reached out and gripped Aveen's shoulder, causing the boy to look up and meet his eyes. "Listen. Are you listening?"

Aveen nodded, the image of an old crone bent-backed, with a hook nose and fingers clawed and reaching for him was squeezed away as the older boy pulled his focus up to his face. Glider looked deeper into him even as he lowered his voice. "She is not going to hurt you. Not unless she needs to. Everyone has a job to do here: the trainers get you ready for combat, Doc Nelson picks up the pieces after they do. But Elisa is different. Her job is to make you see clearly. And sometimes the truth hurts."

Aveen dropped out of the open bay door of the single-seat CVR130 transport and into the blackness. He threw his arms and legs out and glided on the wind that planed smoothly over him as the unmanned drone arced back to the east, the sensation bringing his friend to mind as it always did when he wore the insertion suit. Designed by Glider just before he disappeared, the flight suit with titanium and ceramic mesh webbing running between his wrists and ankles sliced through the air at 10,000 feet as a razor would flesh. The metal lacing through the suit was given additional buoyancy and lift by the magnetic current running through it, and he enjoyed several minutes of flying over a landscape not unlike the one he had toiled on as a boy.

The squares and rectangles of farms were visible from above, and he looked down wondering what the fields were planted with.

VitaSoy, most likely. That gold has got to be MuraWheat.

He left the crops behind as he soared along at 60 kilometers an hour toward the hills ahead. They marked the end of the low country where most of the nation's cereals were grown and the thickening of their masses was parted by a river. This was his primary landmark, and he tightened his stomach and flexed his shoulders as he banked toward the ribbon of water 3,000 feet below. He descended further as he flew over it, curving back and forth until he was only a hundred feet from the surface.

Wonder who would have been the better flier, he mused, his smile behind the black mask of his LT suit slight and more than a little bittersweet. It was a question he knew he could never answer.

Five minutes later he landed with a soft hopping bump and took a few jogging steps to fully stop. His friend and mentor was still on his mind as he pressed the pads on his hips that pulled the extra material into the seams of the LT suit and proceeded to leap lightly from rock to boulder and then to the opposite shore of a narrow section of river. It had reduced to a gurgling stream running between the steep slopes of the hills, and once on the other side, he wondered what Glider's final test would have been.

Not that he would ever know. Glider had been missing for over ten years, and such records were sealed. Aveen had requested to search for him and Elisa when the older *mencist* had disappeared with him into the DOX, but this was denied. Glider and the then 50-something mental scientist had vanished when Aveen was 12, and he hadn't been able to shake his icon from his mind for weeks—months—after that.

Even now, at 23 and about to graduate, the blue-eyed boy who set the bar for all other Cicadas had an iron grip on Aveen's actions. How he led, what techniques he employed, how he saw the world. Even the suit that carried Aveen on the wind which had earned the vanished man his name. Everything was shaped by his lost friend.

And now I am going to graduate, Aveen mused as he saw the lights of the farmhouse a half of a mile up the winding valley. *I wish he could see it. See me become what he meant me to be.*

Aveen crept up the valley, the air quiet and stars bright in the wide river of night sky above him. It was banked on both sides by the dark hills covered in thick stands of oak trees, the pattern broken by the occasional fir. It occurred to him that in daytime, the place must be beautiful; awash in flame and rust, the fall leaves would paint the land with warm color.

"Too good for a traitor to live in," he murmured, pushing away thoughts of gentle breezes and creaking, lazy limbs beneath a blue sky. He kept to the shadows beneath the trees whenever possible, fording into the stream only when he had to. Not that he had to worry about detection. His LT suit made such a possibility remote, although not assured. The form-fitting one-piece bodysuit had advanced dampening technology built into it, hence the name. LT stood for "Light Touch," and was a deceptively simple term. Completely black, the suit muffled sound, absorbed light, and reacted to sudden impacts by distributing the kinetic energy given it in fanlike patterns out from the site.

This made bullets fall to the ground as though they were house flies suddenly knocked unconscious, knives unable to apply enough force to cut, and vicious punches and kicks turn to soft pats. The downside was that of any two-way street; actions and movements too sudden and sharp could see a limb turn rubbery and quick reactions made molasses-slow. The suit was ideal for sniping and heavy weapons fire, however. The recoil of the strongest firearm was made moot by the energy dampening mesh woven into the fabric, so as long as a person could lift the weapon they could fire it.

Aveen had experienced this firsthand when he wielded a rotating pulse cannon at the firing range, a weapon typically mounted on the reinforced frame of a supersonic transport. It weighed a hundred pounds, but that was no real challenge for a top trainee who modeled everything on the academy's standout, if absent, cadet. The recoil would have torn Aveen's arms from their sockets, however. But with the suit, he held the fire steady and eviscerated the brick wall 50 yards ahead of him.

There was no such worry on this mission, however. The only weapon he carried was in the standard operations kit in the tight-fitting bag on his back, and while the .50 caliber Sikkens Manhunter handgun was capable of carving baseball-size holes out of the torso of a target, he didn't need the LT suit to accurately fire it. Thousands of rounds on the center's obstacle courses made such assistance unnecessary. But Aveen wasn't there to make noise; he was there to make a statement. His knife or his hands would speak better as to his abilities than the hand cannon on his back.

The suit made him a shadow moving in the darkness, but Aveen kept his heart rate low and his steps slow. He had no idea what sort of security the target had in place, but considering it was his final exam for promotion to full agent he expected it to be considerable. And yet as he moved along the valley floor, hugging the shores of the river when he could and wading the waters when he couldn't, the absence of tripwires and observation drones linked in a holding pattern around specific rocks and trees made his pulse quicken.

It shouldn't be this easy. The complication Dr. Nelson mentioned must be about to fall.

All he could see was the stars above, shored in by the hills that sloped down to him. All he could hear was the water burbling around his ankles, the gentle croaking of frogs and tinny violins of crickets calling out to each other. The lights of the farmhouse were now only 100 meters ahead, and the calm of the place—the peace—was all wrong. The river continued past the farmhouse to a barn, and Aveen paused in the dark of the trees bordering the stream as he looked over the property.

Main building and two sheds. Large barn twenty to twenty-five paces to the east. No sentries. No observation posts.

Not even a dog guarding the place … it put Aveen, especially on edge. Every other target he had taken over the last six years had been surrounded by seismic, digital, and physical countermeasures. This mission was supposed to be his ultimate challenge, and yet there wasn't even a GMO guarding the place.

Not even an old tick hound looking out for raccoons or wildcats. This is all wrong.

For a thrilling, terrifying moment, Aveen wondered if he had the wrong place. There were several farms and homesteads along the winding course of the river valley, and he struggled to recall the specific details of the one he was meant to go in and eliminate its occupant.

Two-story quarried stone farmhouse with gables. Covered well to the right of the front door. Barn with single large opening approximately 30 meters past it.

It all fit. It was the right place. But nothing else made sense.

And then the front door opened and a silhouette emerged. Aveen tapped his closed eyelids twice, and when he opened them the figure was outlined in pale green. He squinted, and the ocular implants zoomed in. Tiny captions appeared on various parts of the body moving toward the barn: Height 170 centimeters, weight 60 kilograms. Left-handed, 51 years old, slight limp in right leg. It was all correct. The target was who he needed to take out, and was where he was supposed to be.

But how could this man be a threat? That the Protectorate would deem him worthy of private assassination meant he was dangerous. But for being termed as such, he didn't have any protective measures that Aveen could locate. There wasn't even a lock on the gate on the white picket fence around the man's house.

None of this makes sense!

But he rose and lifted the latch on the gate, stepping through with his elbows half bent and palms out in loose claws as he followed the man toward the barn.

BENJI

This is all wrong.

Benji leaned against the wall of the lobby of the hotel and shook his head at the whole business. He had watched the mark for the last hour—watched her chat with two other elderly women in the small cafe on the other side of the lobby. Wearing his scuffed workman's clothes and lounging beside a hover cart of cleaning supplies and maintenance equipment with the posture and disinterest of a wage slave, no one paid any attention or challenged him. But although he was nearly 50 meters away from the cafe and its half dozen small round tables, he could see his target clearly. He watched her laugh with the other two women as they pressed each other to examine the holographic videos of young people running, pirouetting, and waving up from the memdisks on the table between them.

He squinted to magnify the three women at the table, closing the distance to the colorized nanites pouring up from the flat black discs beside their coffee cups and tea trays.

Kids climbing trees. Racing toy boats. Picking flowers.

The images belonged to happy children, as Benji once was before his parents got sick and dreamed their lives away. He had climbed those trees. He had raced boats along the riverbank where wildflowers grew. And now here he was, about to end the life of someone's grandmother.

Why hadn't he died alongside his parents, he wondered, as he watched the women sharing laughter and happy memories. Why hadn't he withered away to a glassy-eyed skeleton as they had, as the soothing corrosive world the virus overlaid onto every moment of waking life took him into oblivion? He could never know the answer any more than he could bring his dead parents back from that undiscovered country.

Aveen said it was the nature of life one night as they lay in their dormitory bunks. "Three men sitting at a bus stop when a car's maglocks go out and it drifts from the lane. It crashes right through the barrier and then through the man on the left. A degree to the right, two men are taken. Another one more, and all three vanish under a ton of plastic and *ferric steel*. Switch it to the car drifting left, and all three go home and tell their kids and wives that God exists."

Benji knew he was right that night in the darkness, with Aveen on the bunk above him and the sounds of sleeping, exhausted cadets all around. When you started to rationalize, to question why, you never found answers that satisfied. Only more doubt, more regret. Better to let things happen because they happen to other people, and leave the questioning for when they happen to you.

Even so, the heavyset woman with the purple shawl and ginger-gray hair fifty paces away didn't strike Benji as someone who thought of life as pointless. She laughed and gestured at her right companion's upturned vase of nanite images, then patted the hand of the woman on the left. She clapped her own hands and clutching them to her as a tiny ballerina made of magnetic memory stepped onto her toes and twirled in place in the center of the table.

This is all wrong, he thought again. *This woman's either a complete psychopath who loves life one minute and plots to end that of millions the next. Or she's just a nice old lady who's sitting around sharing family photos.*

Benji supposed that a person who had resolved to infect their fellow citizens with a contagious terminal disease would be the picture of walking evil. But the image of such a person in his mind wasn't the one sitting there waiting for his knife. He hadn't planned for a cackling hag with a bag full of poisoned red apples, like in the old fairy tales. But the utter absence of anything resembling his expectation of evil in the target made him wonder about the assignment. Not to mention the promised complication Dr. Nelson had mentioned.

But when the old lady's friends stood and waved goodbye, he tensed. He watched the woman with the purple shawl sit alone for several minutes, as he wrestled with his doubt as to whether she was who he was there for. But he could not find a hole in the description provided by Captain Nest's dossier. The old woman with her happy holograms was whom he was there to kill. But as Benji rose, he took his hand from the knife in a sheath inside a seam in his workman's suit. He began walking toward the old woman, who sat smiling down at a little boy napping under a shade tree on a summer's day, his thoughts on how to send her to his parent's country with a minimum of pain.

CELESTE

*C*eleste wore neither a form-fitting black LT suit, nor tradesmen's work clothes as she stepped onto the dance floor of the exclusive party in Bucharest. Her outfit allowed her to blend in as much as the others had, with the distinction being more than a few eyes were on her as she moved. This was the outfit's intention. Should she fail to pull the gaze of those in attendance as she sauntered across the mirror-polished teak floor, her camouflage wasn't doing its job.

Nevertheless, Celeste felt the whole setup was wrong. From the target to the place of execution, nothing about her final mission was as she had imagined it. She looked the part: from her skintight black dress with a high slit up the thigh to show her tanned and muscled legs, and the smooth fabric sliding to and fro across her rounded butt, she was every young man's dream and old man's regret. Using "soft skills" was nothing new in how a mission was performed. And the ballroom where the city's elite celebrated their wealth and power within the bubble provided by the Fence on Bucharest's borders was the type she had infiltrated half a dozen times. But none of those in attendance fit the profile of revolutionaries willing to give their lives to overthrow the government. They just had too much to lose.

She kept her eyes half-closed in the sultry disinterest best suited to getting subjects to misinterpret her intentions and passed through the crowd that eyed her from all sides as she sought her target. Procreation was strictly controlled by the Protectorate, so no one who followed the fluid curves of her should have hoped for the evening to end with her in their bed. But like everything in which a price can be paid, those with means found ways to bend the rules. She counted on it as she slipped between men in expensive black tuxedos and women in silken ball gowns whose colors made up a creamy rainbow of variety, laughing and lightly touching the arms and elbows of those she passed to turn their faces to her.

No target yet. Where is he?

Her outfit seemingly offered no concealment potential for a knife or gun, but in fact weaponized her very sexuality. She wore no bra. This was common enough for the backless dress she wore. But it also allowed her to wear a pair of soft nipple caps which contained a single pill each. All she needed was to locate the target and drop one into his drink, then pretend distress when the poison began to crumple him from within. She could have simply snapped the 53-year-old's neck had she wished, but the lower the profile she kept the better her cover. Even as she wore little cover, attention on her profile was what she sought to cultivate.

She turned out of the main knots of people toward the right side of the room and took a position beside the bar. She was slowly scanning the room with a bored expression that belied her intense consideration, when a voice at her side froze her passing gaze.

"Not enjoying the party either, huh?"

Celeste had to check her swing to the man's throat, covering the action by feigning stretching. As this caused her back to arch and breasts to lift, she didn't worry the man would notice her halted hand strike.

"Yeah, I'm not much for dancing." She lowered her arms and crossed them at the wrists as she leaned on the bar. "But my boss wants me here. So there you are."

"Yes, employers can be so inconsiderate like that," he said, leaning back on his elbows as he looked out on the room. "Such a terrible place to find oneself."

Celeste heard the sarcasm and spared the man a glance. He wasn't who she was there for, and her eyes lingered on him just long enough to verify it before returning to sweep the room.

Mid-30s, expensive suit, touch of gray at the temples.

But what prevented her outright dismissal of him were his hands. The one half-turned toward her was calloused. It was the only one she had seen in the room overflowing with wealth and it was out of place, as were her own callouses. Was he there for her? Was he a Skip looking to break her rhythm and lead her to disaster? Or perhaps the complication Dr. Nelson promised? Another level of challenge on an already stressful assignment?

"Well, I won't keep you," the man said, pushing off from the bar with an easy grace that suggested many hours needed to achieve it. "I'll let you get back to following orders."

He stood looking into the crowd for a few seconds then turned to face Celeste. "But if you ever want to be your own boss, try this." He removed a shimmering rectangle from his coat pocket and placed it on the bar by her right elbow. It caught the light and cast it back as though cut from abalone shell.

She glanced at it with seeming disinterest. "What makes you think I'm looking for a change in careers?"

He smiled. The grin was slight and knowing, and his words shook her. "We all need a change sometimes. Especially when the work we do is done for the wrong reasons. And hurts the wrong people."

He smiled and offered a slight, old-fashioned bow and walked away. Celeste watched him go and then picked up the card. There was nothing on it but the radiating color, and she turned it over to find more of the same.

He wasn't looking to bed me. And he didn't act like he was trying to trap me.

She considered the possibility that she had been made and the man was part of a security detail for one of the room's high rollers. He could have left her a poisoned card whose toxin would be absorbed by her skin several minutes after he walked off and so would have no connection when her body began convulsing and writhing on the floor. It was how she planned to eliminate her own target.

But she wore a monomolecular layer of prophylactic gel on her hands, all the way up to the wrists. It was impermeable, and she had no fear of handling the card. Such precautions were necessary for handling the pills riding on the peaks of her breasts. Otherwise, she would fall beside the target to the floor not long after administering the fatal dose.

But what had he meant by 'hurt the wrong people?' That's not what you say when you're flirting with a stranger at a party. That was personal.

Somehow he had known she was out of place, and possibly even knew what she was there for. This realization sent a surge of adrenaline coursing through her, and she had to fight to keep her bored appearance in place. The man might have been a component of the final test, or a Skip recruiting for one of the mercenary guilds. He might also have just been a guy looking to get laid, who had hit on an eccentric way of getting her attention. Celeste couldn't know, and she was about to toss the card into the trash can behind the bar and go hunt the man down to beat the answer out of him when she caught sight of her target.

A fat man with curly hair and a graying goatee stood looking pleased with himself twenty feet away. He held a glass of champagne, and Celeste breathed a sigh of relief at the knowledge it would be simple to feign a seductive hug and drop a fast-dissolving pill into his drink. But then she noticed the man was arm-in-arm with another man. And it was evident from a few second's consideration they were partners of long and comfortable years.

Celeste frowned. *So much for the dress doing the heavy lifting.*

She felt the card in her hand and looked down at it. After a moment, she slipped it into her purse, then walked toward the pair of men with a bubbly smile in place of the sultry one she arrived with. She would find the man with the calloused hands on her way out. But now it was time for her final job as a Cicada.

5

TOFE

I can't believe this. There has got to be some kind of mistake.

Tofe considered the family sitting beside the pond, his stomach clenching. A father and mother were fishing with their son and daughter on a calm pond as the sun set behind the jagged peaks on the opposite shore, and everything about the scene was perfect for a family gathering. The wind was faint, the breeze gently rustling the leaves of the green trees lining the curving edge of the water. The warmth of the sun sinking behind the Carpathian Mountains three kilometers ahead settled a soft blanket of dimming color over the area. The smells of roast chicken came from the small campfire to the right of the pair of reclining chairs the parents sat in as they watched the boy and girl laugh at each other's efforts—it all made for a pleasant domestic moment.

And I have to slaughter them all.

Tofe couldn't understand—couldn't even remotely conceive—that the people he was sent to kill were these four. And yet the assignment given to him two hours earlier was clear on the

targets for his final exam. He gripped the stock of the Intermit-
tent Phase Plasma Rifle and gritted his teeth, looking at the back
of the boy's head as he lightly jerked his pole to simulate the
twitches of a small silver fish in the water. He could see the curls
of the brown hair and the occasional freckle on the back of his
neck. He could see the smile of the child as he played with the
process of luring swimming sustenance.

God, he's like what, ten? Eleven?

Two hours earlier, Tofe would never have imagined he had to kill
the family laughing and splashing in the beautiful setting. The
assembled group outside the castle each had their own assignment, and no one knew what it was until they boarded their own
transport for fast flights to the testing grounds. But the fact they
would be operating under such conditions made Tofe nervous,
even without knowing the unlikely nature of those he would be
sent to kill.

"I don't know about this," he had muttered, as the group accepted
their packs from a quartermaster and lined up for their respective transport. "What if one of us gets in trouble like on the last
run? We can't help each other if we're apart. I don't even know
where you guys are going."

"Suck it up, chicken little," Celeste grinned, elbowing him before
shouldering her pack. It was far smaller than those of the others,
containing only a dress, poisoned pills, and a few other items. But
she wouldn't know this until on the transport when the magnetic
locks on it opened, along with the decryption of her mission
briefing.

Tofe did likewise, accepting his pack from the granite-jawed troll
of a man, then stepping away to close his eyes and tap the lids
twice. This pulled up the holographic mission briefing, and he
turned and looked at the castle where the setting sun played over

the stones and minarets as he considered the floating writing. It glowed even when overlaid against the rock walls and he shook his head at what he saw.

Werner Kaufman. 49. Accountant. Right-handed. 170 centimeters. 76 kilograms.

The photo showed a middle-aged balding man with a kind expression. This was unusual for the Protectorate ID files, where dour or serious was the norm for the emotions conveyed in a picture for a government card. But the man had smiled, and it unsettled Tofe. It didn't say what he had done to earn a death sentence, nor what sort of defenses would be waiting when his Cicada came to call.

Tofe had no idea who the other members' targets were, nor where, nor what their offense to earn a death sentence had been. And they didn't have any more information in their heads-up displays than he did. The only hint at what Kaufman had done was in the label beneath his photo: "extremist demagogue." It seemed almost an afterthought on the file; an addition placed more for recordkeeping than an offense against the Protectorate worthy of a sentence of silence.

Tofe had stared into the man's faintly smiling expression and felt uneasy.

He looks like someone's kindly uncle, not an anarchist spreading hate and fear.

Not that this was the first such doubt Tofe had felt on the half-dozen missions the team had carried out over the last two years. At least two of the now-dead targets were family men. Fathers whose children would never see them walk through the doors of their homes again. Another had two sisters who needed caring for, and who now had to look after it themselves.

Each of the six targets had rifles or pocket pistols in their hands when the team hit them. This was in direct violation of Protectorate law, and it eased swallowing the justification of putting them down. They had shot back—sometimes shot first—and the desperation and guilt had been clearly written across their faces as they brought their weapons up.

Tofe was still staring at the slight smile of Werner Kaufman when Aveen waved a hand in between Tofe's holographic mission report and the distant fortress the team called home.

"Tofe! You ready to head out?"

Tofe blinked. "Huh? Oh, yeah. Ready."

He closed his eyes on the file which disappeared, and Benji threw an arm over his shoulder.

"One more run and you'll be a man, my son! Time to slip out of our shell and take flight!"

Tofe gave him a tired look. "You don't mean to become agents. You mean the Assignation Ceremony."

"Hey, a man's gotta do what a man's gotta do," Benji said, wiggling his eyebrows up and down with no trace of shame. "And when you've gotta do it with a fine, morally-flexible lady, who couldn't look forward to that?"

Tofe sighed and shook his head, as his friend's arm slipped from his shoulder. "Yeah. Nothing like a little murder for foreplay to get in the mood."

Celeste rolled her eyes and stepped up, her transport settling down on a cushion of magnetized air twenty paces in front of her. "If we're sent to a person's door, odds are they did something to call us there. Keep your head down and your eyes open. Do your job, and you'll be fine."

"I notice you didn't say anything about keeping my mind open," he said as she walked toward the unmanned supersonic craft that would carry her to her own site of human destruction. He watched her slip into the seat and the small ship take off, then gripped the strap of his pack and walked toward his own after it settled onto the landing pad.

And now here he was, looking down the laser-assisted sight of a rifle that would pulverize a tunnel through the skull of the kindly man in the photo. His family would not hear the shot, as the bolt of superheated plasma wouldn't make a sound as it destroyed their husband and father. But they would see his body with its staring eyes afterward. They might even be looking at him when the shot cut through.

And I can't leave witnesses, he sighed, as he shifted the focus to the back of the mother's head. *It's one thing to leave a panicked crowd milling around a body in a mall or park. But they know Kaufman. They share his name, and there's a chance he's told them some of his secrets.*

He watched them for several minutes, his eyes extending through the scope to trace their bodies minutely, to examine and judge a thousand tiny and seemingly insignificant details. How they walked, whether they made eye contact with each other and of which types, how they tended the fire, how they treated both the fish they caught and the bait they used. It was what Captain Nest had hammered into every cadet: the devil's in the details.

And despite his most focused attention and with each movement of not only the father but his entire family, Tofe couldn't detect a demon within any of them.

And yet he couldn't just pack up and walk away. There had been many examples over the years of his training that people could and would sustain covers, even when not in the areas they were attempting to infiltrate. It was possible that Kaufman and the others were all just totally committed to their respective roles. Or that he was, and they had been left in the dark.

Tofe let out a long breath and sighted along the spine of the man, slowly raising the barrel until the red laser dot was in the center of his head. He spared a last look at the happy family with their sunset, campfire, and fish, and made his choice.

6

NO GOOD DEED GOES UNPUNISHED

The next morning the room was once more filled with cadets. The mood, however, was entirely different. No one laughed; there was no joking or snide comments about anyone's performance. All were serious. All were changed by what they had experienced the evening before.

Captain Nest considered the room. She had seen squads go through this change and knew their feelings well. She had been through the training ten years earlier and still remembered the man she had killed. She had gone through the hell of it and came out the other side. Now she stood before them to prepare those heading into it and help steel the resolve of those who had been through it.

"I'm glad to see you all in attendance this morning," she said, nodding at several of the cadets to impose the sense of individualized attention. "I know that some of you came back injured and with great difficulty. But that only goes to prove the value of our training and the resolve to see the mission accomplished."

The men and women she nodded at bore bandages over cheeks. Burns and lacerations across hands and other visible parts of skin were also present. None showed evidence of crying or the sharp intake of breath which accompanied a stab of pain from cracked ribs when they moved. She noticed the absence of these signs, and within her approved.

"Only Cadet Tofe Regis was unable to join us this morning. He sustained more extensive injuries and is recuperating in Dr. Nelson's clinic. But I have every assurance his wounds will be only a temporary inconvenience, and he will return to us ready to engage in the greater mission all of you will be a part of."

"Ahem."

Nest spun to find a smaller man standing in the doorway with his hands held behind his back. She hadn't heard it open; but then, General Aepal had passcodes to override the door's chimes.

And he does like to make an entrance.

The general entered the room still clutching his hands behind him and the section of wall slid soundlessly back in place. As it did, all cadets rose to their feet, and within a few seconds, all stood at attention. Nest greeted her commander with a stiff salute that every trainee followed.

"General Aepal," she said, lowering her hand as the rest of the room did likewise. "I did not know you would be joining us."

The man who entered was several inches shorter than her, and yet he walked with the casual grace that came from long command. His uniform was spotless, his beard neatly trimmed and impressive. The mustaches curled slightly up at the tips and the gray and silver of it all imparted an impression of wisdom. The eyes twinkled showing keen intelligence. But they also suggested great observation. More than one cadet had the feeling their leader knew everything they tried to hide behind their eyes, and few met his gaze for long. This man missed nothing, and the fatherly, friendly demeanor did not reach his eyes.

"I wanted to be here to celebrate the graduation of our latest crop of cadets," the general noted, staring slowly around the room and nodding at several people as he smiled. "I reviewed the syncs of your assignments and looked over the reports you all turned in. Most impressive."

Captain Nest felt a swell of pride within her at these words, knowing her superior and surrogate father did not hand out compliments lightly.

However, the celebratory sensation withered within her in the next moment.

"Unfortunately," he said, the smile disappearing into his beard and the twinkling eyes turning hard, "not all of you will be progressing. Two of you did not meet the minimum requirements for Agent status from your final test yesterday evening."

The atmosphere of the room shifted. A chill seemed to fill the space, although the climate-controlled system which allowed filtered and recycled air into the space would not have provided it. This was purely emotional. And all cadets sitting around the two ringed circles felt the thrill of terror slither up their spines.

"Cadet Thompson and Cadet Vreeland," General Aepal said, his eyes moving from one woman to a man. "Come down here."

The 23-year-old female and 22-year-old male did so, rising from their respective rings on the lower table and came to stand before their commanding officer. They stood at attention and their expressions were blank. But a tremble could be seen in the left hand of the man, and the woman's right eye twitched. General Aepal considered the pair for half a minute without speaking.

Then he opened his mouth and addressed the room, not looking at the two cadets.

"In times of war it is easy to lose one's way. It is human to feel compassion and normal to feel doubt. But war is also the time to transcend these considerations. Murder is illegal in peacetime. It is required in war. But what marks a "good person" when guns are silent and diplomacy rules has little place when cannons are firing and civilians choke on poison gas and dream themselves into oblivion." He motioned to the two without looking at them. "These two individuals standing before you could not make the transition from one to the other. They could not allow themselves to fully join the reality of war. They allowed their targets to evade termination, and so have endangered us all."

He pulled a small plastic controller from his coat pocket and clicked it at the large white disk on the floor. Smoky nanites began to filter out of it as he went on speaking.

"Random one-shot camera drones were included in several of the transports you used last night. After you left the transports they were released to follow, and they monitored your runs and relayed the data back to us in real time."

The smoke took shape and the outlines of small stalls with numerous humanoid shapes followed. Within a few seconds everything took on the colorized detail of a night market: bolts of cloth, jars of dried fruits and spices, *memdisks*, and other electronic wares all shared space with dozens of other items and services. The female cadet was seen walking through, her outfit casual and without anything to suggest she carried a weapon, or was looking to use it on someone.

"Cadet Thompson successfully identified the target," Aepal explained, his tone that of an instructor narrating a mildly interesting educational video for a semi-caring class, "and managed to isolate the person. This was all by the book, and nothing to critique."

The nanite version of Thompson and the wizened old rare book-seller stood in the back corner of the man's shop, and she could be seen holding a short curving blade.

"Where Cadet Thompson failed was because of what happened next."

The two figures were talking, with the little old man cowering back from her. But instead of raising the knife she lifted her other hand and pointed toward the shop's back door. The book-seller turned and ran, and Thompson watched him go. Then she slipped the knife back into the folds of her clothing and turned and walked out of the front door.

"She let the target go."

Aepal said it simply and without emotion. There was no anger in his voice, nor condemnation.

He repeated the review of Vreeland's recording of the male cadet allowing a woman to escape from him in a city park after speaking with her, then clicked the nanites to sift back into the white platform.

The general looked each of the two in the eye, going from one to the other and back again. "In time of war extraordinary measures are required. And no cause is lost until it is won. But it is if one gives in to the enemy. Turn and face your former colleagues."

They did so, and the room looked back with a tenseness that was palpable. No one spoke; there was nothing to say. All understood that these two would not be graduating along with them. But how they were drummed out of the service was something that shocked even Nest.

"Take a good long look at the price of failure. Understand that I take no pleasure in this, nor should any of you have reason to fear a similar outcome so long as you carry out your assignments. Let this be your final lesson as cadets: the price of freedom is high, and only those who are willing to pay it deserve to be the ones to provide it."

Without another word he pulled his sidearm from his right hip and lifted it to the back of the head of the woman. One quick shot and his arm swung the side of the head of the man, who had half-turned in response to the bolt of plasma burning through the skull of the woman on his left. The bolt of blue-hot energy tunneled its way through him and buried itself in the far wall, and both former cadets teetered for a moment before crumbling to the floor.

The room was too shocked by the executions to immediately respond, but General Aepal did not give them the opportunity. He holstered his sidearm and called out to the four nearest cadets on the outer table ring. "Come here and carry the bodies to the Infirmary. They will be given a funeral of honor and their bodies returned to their families. Necessarily, they will be cremated prior to doing so. Their families will know the truth that we provide them: that they died serving their country in order to protect those who could not protect themselves."

The three men and one woman who stood and came over to pick up the bodies, one person on each side of the corpses, carried stern expressions as they did so. Nest's jaw nearly cracked with the pressure she applied to it as she struggled to keep her mouth shut as she watched them lift the lifeless bodies and carry them through the door that once more silently opened. Aepal turned to her, and she forced the grim look from her face.

"I trust that you have no questions, Captain?"

She returned his gaze without blinking. It took her a moment to answer so that her voice was even. "No sir."

He nodded. "Good. Then assemble the teams and brief them on their roles. I sent the files to your E-office." She saluted and he turned to leave, pausing on the threshold of the open section of the wall.

"The motto of the Special Activities Circle is *exoritur verum*," he said with his head half-turned back to the room. "You all know it means 'truth rises,' and it is more than a slogan to us. But you only know the truth we've told you. Your mission to the DOX will give you the rest of it. There you will see why I have to take such measures despite the loathing I feel for doing so."

He left, the door once more closing to leave the wall smooth and without feature. The continuity was broken by the opposite side, however. There the stench of burnt plastic and fried metal emanated out from the twin trickles of smoke curling up from the golf ball-sized holes in the wall where his killing shots had penetrated.

The room was silent for a long minute, then Nest cleared her throat.

"The rest of you will be searching the DOX for the secret weapon of the Resistance. Your orders are to locate the item and retrieve it if possible, destroy it if necessary. Whether you return yourselves is immaterial. All that matters is the elimination of this weapon from the hands of the rebels. And after the demonstration the General just provided," Nest said, her voice tight, "I think we all can understand the stakes of this mission. Even I am not privy to all of the details, and you will be given less. But suffice it to say that this item is important enough that we cannot have anything less than perfect obedience from those who are sent to retrieve it. Any questions?"

7

THE WORLD SECURITY COUNCIL

*G*eneral Aepal stepped into his office, his expression heavy. He did feel loathing at killing the two cadets, but it couldn't be helped. There was too much at stake.

He went to his desk and laid his right hand on a square pad. It glowed, and he spoke to the air: "Secure the room. Director override. Aepal, Nicolas J."

The room darkened and the wall where the door was glowed with its outline in a soft red light. He removed his hand and spoke again. "World Security Council."

The white disk on the floor in the center before the desk was the same as that in the cadet briefing room, and it glowed as a stream of nanites poured upward. Soon a line of seated men and women appeared, all looking back at him as he walked from his desk to stand before them.

A woman near the middle spoke. "Good morning, general. I take it the leak has been plugged?"

Aepal nodded. "Yes. I just saw to it personally."

The heads nodded and murmured. "Good," a man beside her in the holographic conference said. He looked to the right and left. "I take it any such breaches were also seen to on your end?"

Several people answered they had. The man nodded at this and returned his gaze to Aepal. "The final test always has a few. But we've never seen so many at one time. Regardless, we must move forward. Are we ready for Phase Two?"

"Yes," Aepal said, removing the controller from his pocket and clicking. A second haze of nanites wafted out of the white disk and took on a series of intelligence reports. "The rebels have nearly completed the substance, although it cannot be definitively determined how near they are to a weaponization state. Our new crop of agents will be deployed to the DOX in a week to seek it out. They will be told it is an updated version of the plague which initiated the worldwide pandemic 30 years prior, a pathogen we're calling *entropy*. Therefore, all of the agents expect to have to deal with toxic substances, and they won't look too closely at what they're dealing with. I assume the rest of you will state similar precautions to your own teams?"

The heads nodded.

"Good," Aepal said, using his hands to highlight several floating files. "That was the issue with several of the cadets on our respective runs. Conscience got the better of them, and they made the mistake of interrogating the targets. Most of them knew very little to start with. But it was enough for the cadets to realize they were not all hard-core members of the rebellion. We need them to similarly not look too carefully at the substance once they've retrieved it. If they only know the fear we've raised them to believe in, like the population at large for the last three decades, we have no reason to believe the operation will fail."

"Ironic that the weapon they're seeking to destroy is actually the cure for *dreamscape*," the Amazonian minister mused. "An irony worthy of the drama."

"I prefer nonfiction," a large woman with a gravelly voice noted, a smirk in her tone. "But then you Latins always were suckers for empty passion."

"And you Canadians wear the mask of good will to the world," he replied, his tone cool. "And yet you have more than your share of bodies to answer for."

"Enough," a man said from the far end of the dais before Aepal could step between the two. "The reclamation of the cure is only part of what must occur. The mission to apprehend the scientist who provided it must also be addressed."

"And it is being seen to," Aepal said, turning to the man who had spoken. "I have already selected a team to collect the individual in question."

"Can we rely on them?" a slender, smooth-toned woman asked, her voice tinged with a Russian accent.

"They are the ones who overcame the alarm in the hotel two days ago. They completed their assignment and got to the extraction point without exposure. They will collect Dr. Jiang."

"And the individual who attempted to expose them?" the Amazonian minister asked.

"That person seemed to be testing our capabilities more than anything," Aepal answered. "Otherwise they would have fought the team assassinating the target, or at the least to extricate the individual themselves before my people arrived, so as to prevent it."

The room seemed to feel this was sufficient, but one silhouette cleared his throat. "So this mercenary is in the wind, fine. But I wonder if we are pushing the cadets too hard. They have only just achieved agent status. Physical and psychological wear and tear is inevitable, and if they are not in optimum condition, they may fumble assignments we cannot allow them to fail. Specifically the *entropy* mission. Why do we not simply use older, more experienced agents?"

Aepal sighed as he brought up different files, telling the room he had sent them to their E-offices for review. "The previous class of agents was my initial group of choice. But they suffered some lingering effects from time in the DOX. None died, but also none of them have finished having their minds corrected and blood exchanged. Following that, Dr. Nelson tells me it will be at least a month before their physical therapy is complete. Then they will be both at full capacity and immune to *dreamscape*, but we cannot wait that long. Clarion is moving, and my people tell me they will implement the cure in under a week if we don't intercept it."

8

THE PRICE OF DREAMS

*D*r. Nelson was standing with his back to the clinic's only occupied bed when a voice from it made him turn.

"I thought those things were illegal. But seeing as how you're so close to the general, I suppose exceptions can be made."

Nelson turned from the row of Plexiglas containment spheres, cubes, and rectangles to look at the bed's occupant, and smiled. "No, I suppose it's more the albatross around my neck to remind me of past mistakes than a show of power. Conversely, it also offers hope for a greatly overpopulated, and far too turbulent, world."

The items in question were in the series of compartments of different sizes, with some moving and others stationary. Some appeared to be plants, while others were clearly animals. But just what kind of animals and what species of plant, was very much open to interpretation. And in some cases, the line between the two was blurred.

Are these all mutates from the DOX?" Tofe asked, sitting up and leaning forward. Nelson eyed him, noting the slash across the left side of his head that caused concussion was almost completely healed. The other scrapes and bruises were already gone, and Nelson stepped over and flicked a penlight in front of his eyes several times as he continued speaking.

"Yes. They're all the result of the *dreamscape* plague. But they aren't contraband," he added, switching off the light and returning it to his lab coat's pocket and stepping back. "They're part of the cure for the disease. Or at least I hope they are."

Tofe sat up with a wince. "But why are they all here? They weren't the last time I was."

Nelson acknowledged this with a small shrug. "Lack of space for one, desperation for another. We've had no cure even after three decades of the best efforts from the best minds." He sighed as he looked at a yucca-like plant with faintly glowing bulbous purple fruits. "General Aepal had shifted his attention from curing the disease to containing it, so it will burn itself out. And so my pet project of testing the *divergents* was underfunded. As in: It was completely cut off. So I house them here, continuing my experiments in the hopes of stumbling upon some variant in genes or adaptation that might be spliced onto the human genome. A true cure is what I'm after, but I'll settle for a workable vaccine."

"An ounce of prevention?" Tofe asked, giving the doctor a wry look.

Nelson smiled. "Indeed. And considering how *dreamscape* interacted with non-mammalian and even botanical species," he added, as Tofe left the bed and struggled to his feet, "there is every reason to hope the solution is right there in the altered genetic codes of these subjects."

"Where did they come from?" Tofe asked, as he walked slowly over to stand before the row of polished plastic cages.

"The agents, mostly," Nelson said, moving to stand beside him. "They would find them out in the DOX from time to time, and they knew I wanted them. So they brought them to me if they could."

"That *violet pendry* is one of the largest I've seen."

The older man raised his eyebrows. "You know it?"

Tofe grimaced at the gently waving plant with the bulging purple pods. "Yeah. We've met."

The older man considered him for several seconds, then turned back to the aberration. "I wasn't aware cadets had much time for chimero-botanical studies."

"We don't," Tofe said, going right up to the glass and peering in from a few inches away. "And even if we did, the library is, shall we say, a little light on such reading materials."

Nelson watched him with interest. "How do you know about this species, then? And more to the point, why should you care?"

"Hunger always makes you care about what's around you," Tofe replied, his eyes on the plant with an expression Nelson couldn't name. "You always want to know whether it's good to eat, is edible, or just how much you can take before its poison makes the bark or fruit not worth the trouble."

Nelson blinked, his mind whirling. "Wait, you ate it? That means your family was one of the... I'm sorry. I can't remember the term—"

"The *withered*," Tofe said quietly, his tone hardening as he kept his eyes on the plant. "The infection put them into the *dreamtime*, and they never came out. I kept my brother alive by hunting and gathering. Scavenging, mostly. But we ate."

"What dreams did your parents have?"

Nelson asked the question before he could stop himself, and before he could answer he apologized. "I'm sorry. Sometimes I can be tactless. I just so rarely get to interview someone who had firsthand experience living in the DOX."

Tofe shrugged. "Forget about it. It was another life."

The older man had the impression that the event which the injured agent went on to describe was so much a part of him and yet so distant, that he could no longer feel the wound of it. The scar was there, but the hurt was buried so long as to be impossible to pull back to the surface. And Tofe went on speaking.

"We grew up on the coast. A little village called Riale. You wouldn't know it; no one does today, and there's no one alive there now. My father fished, and my mother kept house. She's who I learned about plants from. He taught me about the sea." Tofe continued to stare into the glass box, but Nelson could tell that his eyes were not seeing it. He was looking far back into his childhood, to a time before the training and the assassinations. Back to when he was just a boy on the coast gathering herbs and helping his father pull in nets.

"I don't know about other people," he said. "I don't know if they dream in the same way. But my parents got lost in their real lives. My father stumbled out of the house to his skiff and off to the rolling seas to continue to fish, even though he was only dreaming of doing it. My mother talked to the plants she gathered. Talked to them like she used to talk to my brother and I. It was..." he swallowed, and Nelson saw his left eye twitch. "It was hard."

Nelson took a moment before speaking, and when he did his words were soft. "I can imagine."

Tofe took a breath and cleared his throat as the buried scar moved toward the surface. "Yeah. To see both of them still living the lives they did to take care of us, but they couldn't see we were there. They had forgotten we existed. My mother dreamed of a plant kingdom. She saw Alice in Wonderland, with the talking flowers and all that. My father lived through clear days and storms, empty nets and bursting ones. Gods of the sea and monsters of the deep. Whatever the weather actually was and if he caught fish or not, that is what he perceived. To him, everything was about the boat and the sea. There was nothing for me or my brother, or even my mother. That was what the disease really took from me. That's what you took from me," he said, turning to look Nelson in the eye.

The black man was so focused on hearing the dreams of the sickened people that at first he missed what Tofe said. Then he blinked and took a step back. "You—you know?"

Tofe stared at him for several seconds without replying, his expression hard. "Like I said: When you're hungry, you want to know all you can about what will bring you relief. My parents went insane and tried to take my brother and I with them. So I wanted to know why. It wasn't hard to find out where the virus originated from—the government told us Clarion did it. All it took was reading the papers to see where it was spreading and work backwards. And when I figured out where the government's biochemical weapons division was headquartered, I just had to look up who the scientists were in the field that the virus was. It was just two people: you and Dr. Guozhi Jiang. And he's dead."

Nelson swallowed, a trickle of sweat dribbling down from his right temple and his heart thudding painfully. "Yes. Yes, he died five years ago. Cancer."

"How do you know?"

It was a simple question and it made Nelson frown. "Well, he was relocated to another department just before he got sick. We tried to keep in touch; both of us were determined to find a cure for what we'd made. But he kept working even as the cancer ate him from inside. I never got to visit him before the disease took him," he added, his eyes dropping.

Tofe watched the man for another few seconds then looked back to the plant.

"I watched them dream their lives away over those six months. It never infected my brother and I, though. Sometimes I wanted it to," he said, his voice growing softer. "I think it would have been easier. To not worry about anything; not remember anything. To just slip into whatever dream world the virus gave me, and wither to dust."

He half-turned back to Nelson. "You know that's why they're called 'withered,' right? Because the dreams cut them off from reality, even to the point they don't eat or drink."

Nelson swallowed, his stomach churning as his guilt intensified. But Tofe looked back to the plant and continued speaking, not giving him a chance to comment.

"But my brother needed me, and my parents did too. I was only twelve and he was seven, and together we kept my parents eating and drinking. I did, really. Forced them to, or tricked them by playing to their dream at the time. But it couldn't last for too long, and it didn't. I couldn't catch fish with him in a boat. He would flail around fighting imaginary sea monsters or rogue waves. She heard the cutting of herbs or the pulling of plants as if they were babies crying out in pain. If I gathered plants, I did it when she wasn't there. If I fished, I had to do it at night when he was properly asleep."

He was quiet for half a minute before Nelson asked what had happened to them in the end.

"I came back one evening just before sunrise with a couple of fish to find my parents both dead. He thought that the seaweed had become tangled in his nets and he was tearing it from the webbing when she caught him. I don't think she could have heard him pulling up the plants, as the seaweed was by that point dry and fairly inconsequential. But maybe the sound of him wrestling with the nets was enough. Maybe he roared at them as though they were tentacles wrestling his catch back into the water. Either way, she must have thought her precious flowers and vines were under attack. And so she protected them as any mother would. So they fought, and she caught him in the neck with a gaff hook, and he pulled her into the surf in a bear hug. As he bled out, she drowned."

Nelson lifted a hand and reached out to grasp the younger man's shoulder in consolation. His fingers hovered in the air for a moment, then he withdrew them to let his hand fall to his side. "For what it's worth, and I don't imagine it's worth much, but I am truly sorry."

The glimmering line traced down Tofe's left cheek as Nelson said this, and Tofe did not wipe it away. He did not blink, or acknowledge the tear. Instead he asked if Nelson had ever lost anyone.

The old scientist sighed and nodded. "Yes, a long time ago when I was twenty. I had been drafted into the Protectorate's army—123rd regiment of the southern Carpathian infantry. But when they learned I had been pulled out of a bioengineering degree at the University of Leipzig, they reassigned me to the chemical and biological weapons division. The same one you found me in all those years later."

He removed a pair of faintly-glimmering gloves from a drawer that he pulled on, and whose upper ends reached above his elbows. He took up a plastic jug of small brown pellets and a scoop, and began walking along the row of cages.

"It was a position that allowed me to see the bigger picture of things, and for a time I felt like I was making a good contribution. The world had fallen into chaos, and every family was at risk and every civilization teetering on the brink." He scooped out a small amount of pellets and reached through a round section of one of the Plexiglas cages. The disk his hand parted was the size of a basketball and flared in blue-white light as the scoop passed through. He deposited the pellets in a dish a few feet away from what looked like a turtle who had bathed in a rainbow, then withdrew his arm.

"There was no *dreamscape* then," he said, as he walked down the line of pens and ladled pellets into several. "Just the same timeless misery of one part of humanity seeking to crush another part."

Tofe's jaw hardened and his eyes narrowed as he looked at the old man. "I didn't ask you for your hero's journey to being the savior of the Protectorate. I asked you if you lost anyone."

Nelson nodded and sighed. "Yes, I'm sorry. I should have just come out and said it. My cure killed my own brother and parents."

Tofe turned to look at him, surprise and disbelief on his face. "They were *dreamers*?"

Nelson nodded and the hurt he felt at recalling the loss showed more on his face than it had with the younger man. "I thought they would be safe. I didn't realize that the virus could become airborne. I didn't know that it could be transmissible after the subject had expired, or that it could jump between species. Guozhi didn't think it could, either. But that's how they got it. My parents and brother volunteered at the hospital, caring for the sick and dying. I convinced them not to work in the ER or admissions where there was the greatest risk of exposure."

He felt the old twist in his stomach at the guilt he was sharing. And while he wanted to stop, to just push it down as he had spent the last three decades trying to do on a daily basis, it still bubbled up. It flared in his guts and choked him. But the pain he had forced on Tofe and countless other children brought a wash of shame that overflowed his own sense of failure. And he pressed on.

"They catalogued the effects and final messages of the deceased," he said, his hands shaking as he returned the jug and scoop to the drawer. He withdrew a three-liter bottle with a long sprayer connected to a hose and started back down the line of cages, reaching in to deposit a mist of silvery liquid onto the plants he had not offered pellets. "Many people who became ill realized that they had little time, and so they would write letters or put a holographic farewell on a memdisk. My parents and brother would catalog these and try to get them to the next of kin. But it also meant that they had to be around the bodies of the deceased. Guozhi and I had engineered the virus to only be viable within a living host. We never thought it could infect someone after that person had passed on."

He nodded at the plant Tofe had said he and his brother ate. "And I certainly never anticipated that it could jump from humans to a non-mammalian species." He sighed up at the ceiling. "I was wrong about a great many things in my youth, and I've spent the last three decades trying to make up for it."

Tofe's expression was thoughtful as he looked into the glass box Nelson sprayed. "So you created *dreamscape* as a weapon, with the idea it would end the war. It got way out of your control and screwed up everything outside the mag fields of the Protectorate zones. Turned plants and animals sideways and backwards on their evolutionary paths and added more than a few new branches to the trees of the whole system. And what you created killed your own family."

He suddenly squeezed his eyes shut and laid a hand on the side of his head, then swooned and almost fell. Nelson caught him and gripped him from the side, turning him toward the bed.

"You need to rest. You had a pretty serious bleed, and I alleviated the pressure with a laser trepanation. It'll heal soon enough, but you've got to give it the chance to do so."

He led Tofe back to bed and settled him into it, the medical emergency temporarily pushing aside the old feelings that churned his stomach, then stood and made to walk away. A hand slipped out from the bedcovers and gripped his left wrist. Nelson looked back in surprise and Tofe's eyes were clear as he looked up him. "I'm sorry for your loss, too. What that's worth, I don't know. But I don't blame you. Or Dr. Jiang."

He released Nelson's wrist and sank back on the bed. They said nothing for the next half-minute, and the doctor returned to his chores of feeding the collection of captive aberrations. "These subjects from the DOX … " He looked back at Tofe, his expression showing the barest trace of hesitancy. "I'd like to hear your experiences with the *divergents*. It might help."

Tofe considered the man and his request, then nodded. "Yeah, all right. Just wheel me around in a chair so I don't faceplant as we go."

Nelson nodded and returned to the bedside pushing along a levitating chair which Tofe struggled into. He leaned back and the chair dipped a few inches to compensate, then Nelson rested a hand on the back and pushed it along until they stood in front of the rows of glass cages. "Where do you want to start?"

Tofe looked along the line. "Let's go to that night swan. I've always wanted to see one up close."

Nelson pushed him to stop before the three-by-five box where a large black bird lay dozing with its face tucked into the crease of its left wing. It breathed easily in sleep and did not stir when the men talked just outside of its pen.

"Yes, it's of particular interest," Nelson said, eyeing the bird with shining eyes. "It's the only animal I've encountered which is both free of and captured by the *dreamscape* virus. At night the infection takes over, and the bird is trapped within the hallucinations of the illness. But it shrugs them off in the day. How it does this, I haven't been able to determine."

Tofe slid his hands along both sides of the chair and it glided forward to within a foot of the cage. The bird stirred and raised its head, looking up to meet his eye. The black marbles met his blue ones, and Nelson felt as though something passed between them.

"I always looked for them when I was out hunting," Tofe said, his voice soft as he and the bird connected. "They made no noise when flying, but I could hear when they landed on the water. The splash was just over a whisper, but I heard it. My brother and I would try to creep up and see them when they left the sky. We did, sometimes. But never this close. He was why we worked so hard to get close. I would have tried to shoot it, or trap it. But he wouldn't let me."

Nelson looked at the bird. "Why? What made the swan special to him?"

"It was because of the old fairy tale. The *Minciuna ascunsă*. He always loved them, and it was his favorite. Of course, we never saw a leprechaun at the end of a rainbow, nor a woman in a tower whose hair was the way to reach her. But the black bird was real. And he always prayed we'd be the ugly ducklings who would one day fly away from it all as swans. Me? I couldn't see anything but Hansel and Gretal. Just a couple of kids starving in the woods while their parents were far away."

Nelson sighed. "I read those old stories to my daughter when she was little. Back at the beginning of the Separation, there was still the chance to live normally." He smiled, the expression bitter-sweet. "She wouldn't sleep until I read her something from the Brothers Grimm or Hans Christian Anderson. She liked *The Ugly Duckling*. But it wasn't her favorite."

Tofe looked from the bird to him. "What was?"

"*The Little Mermaid*." He let out a breath as the bird looked at him. "Maybe she and your brother had something in common."

"What do you mean?"

Nelson looked at the shiny round eyes of the black bird. "Both stories are about being dissatisfied with what you were. Both were about trying to escape what you were born into."

Tofe looked back at the swan. "She died, didn't she?"

Nelson tried to answer but his throat closed on the words. He swallowed, and spoke a moment later. "Yes. She was killed."

He did not elaborate and Tofe didn't press him. He merely sighed and nodded. "My brother was, too. At least, I think he was."

Nelson looked up. "You aren't sure?"

Tofe shook his head. "He disappeared one day after my parents died." He sighed and looked at the bird, then reached out and laid a hand softly on the glass. "I like to think he flew away like his swan. That they took to the air and got far above all of this."

They didn't talk any more after that. The old doctor puttered around tending to various duties, living and administrative, and Tofe accompanied him. Finally, the younger man's head began to throb, and Nelson helped him back to bed. Once Tofe was asleep with the help of a sedative, Nelson took a look around the room before moving to the door. He looked to the bird in its glass cage and found it staring at him. It met his gaze unblinking, then returned its head to beneath its wing.

Nelson watched the soft rise and fall of the oil-black feathers for a few heartbeats, then switched off the light and closed the door.

9

LOVE REDUCED TO A PUNCHLINE

*A*veen and Celeste crouched in the shadows across the street from the six-story apartment building in a suburb of Bucharest. The night was deeper than usual, owing to the blackout order keeping cities dark so as to preserve energy. This conveniently occurred whenever agents had an operation in the immediate area, but the disinformation released by the Ministry of Public Awareness ensured that there was always a supposedly random collection of municipalities which had to abide by it.

Only the streetlamps were powered, and they cast ghostly pyramids of ivory light down through the thick, humid air hovering over the still day-warmed streets. It made both new agents sweat in their LT suits in the shadows of a pair of buildings on their side of the road, and Celeste blinked and turned her head at a distant flickering off to her right. A low groan sounded shortly afterward, and she clicked her tongue softly as the mountains returned to darkness after the lightning expelled their energy into the clouds.

"Storm's coming."

Aveen grunted as he finished assembling his sniper's rifle. "Weather report gives us a window of an hour. More than enough time to get in and out."

She watched him slide the scope along the top of the barrel until it clicked into place.

"Surprised we got this assignment. Thought they'd send a more senior team."

Aveen slapped a magazine into the base of the rifle and laid the long black weapon on its side on a dark rectangular cloth within easy reach. "We're agents now. If we couldn't handle this, they wouldn't have assigned it. You getting cold feet?"

She made a face and punched his shoulder. She wasn't trying to hurt him, but it didn't matter. The suit dampened her blow to the point he didn't even shift his position. "Say that again when we're in a combat sim, true believer."

He grinned and was about to say something when a small green light on his right wrist flashed in a slow sequence. It appeared on her wrist as well and his face became serious. "All right. It's showtime."

Celeste followed his gaze up along the side of the building on the opposite side of the street, her lenses compensating for the gloom. Everything appeared in soft surfaces and outlines of green: the road with its maglocked shutters running in a long line to the right and left, the cars parked at angles or parallel depending on how near they were to the intersections. The apartment buildings were the most prominent feature in the wash of green against the city night. Most were ten stories tall and crafted in the Brutalism style adopted following the Plague War. All hard and heavy, with little in the way of adornment, the square columns of concrete six to ten stories tall provided a sense of immovable strength. The plague hadn't resulted in howling, aggressive Dreamers who assaulted any occupied spaces as the initial fears suggested. But the architecture channeling a medieval castle gave people comfort in any case.

Celeste stared up at the forest of uncaring stone on all sides that glowered down at the pair beneath the cloudless and starry sky. The agents of the Romanian Protectorate lived in an actual castle, and while ancient it was far more charismatic than anything the new age offered. *Modern, but I wouldn't want to live here*, Celeste thought, her eyes tracing the apartments.

The green light ceased blinking and Aveen pressed his fingertips to his throat where his commlink was implanted. "We're set to go in on our end. Benji and Tofe?"

The reply came after a pause with Tofe speaking in Celeste's right ear where the audio implant wrapped around her auditory nerve like a cozy octopus. "Yep, we're in position."

"All right," Aveen said, "sending the unlocked packet now."

He placed his fingers onto his left wrist and a holographic panel appeared. He typed a few buttons and each of his fellow agents' wrists began to glow. A file appeared above them a moment later and all examined it. A minute later Aveen spoke.

"The plan is simple, so let's keep it that way. The target is Dr. Jieshi Yang. Surveillance has determined he's being kept on the 5th floor, in apartment E."

Aveen typed a command and nanites poured up to take on the shape of an older Asian man in a white lab coat. He wore glasses and stood slightly hunched, his posture pulled down by his large stomach. The same figure emerged from the left wrists of the rest of the team.

Tofe's voice murmured in Celeste's ear. "Extraction or elimination?"

"E-trac," Aveen said, as the man began to slowly rotate above each of their wrists. "We get him out and a transport will meet us on the roof to fly him home. It'll be a skyhook, so I hope nobody had a big dinner."

"Home?" Benji asked. "He's one of ours?"

Aveen looked down at the transparent figure. "Yes. Dr. Yang is an infectious disease specialist who was kidnapped from a Protectorate facility nearly a year ago. They've been hunting all over the country for him, and data taps on known Clarion associates finally revealed that he was inside the building across the street."

Benji snorted. "No wonder we couldn't find him. He wasn't in some DOX cave out in the wastes. He was in our own backyard."

"Yes," Aveen said, tapping the button to end the shared holographic image. The figure vanished and all of their wrists went dark. "He was working on sequencing the genetic information of *dreamscape* in various species when they took him. Plants, mammals, avian. They hoped he would be able to cook up an even more virulent version of the virus based on combining his research subjects, and we have to get him back. The hope is he can turn the tables and give us a lot of intel on Clarion's operations."

Celeste eyed the street in both directions, her thoughts on the mission's possible complications. She wasn't worried she would run into another weird man dropping business cards and pearls of wisdom. But with such a valuable target inside the building across the road from her and Aveen, there would be guards. And rescues rarely went off without violence.

"Company at 3 o'clock," Tofe murmured in their ears.

She and Aveen looked to their right. The road was deserted, and at first she couldn't understand what had caught his attention.

Then she saw them. Through white cones of halogenic light the lamps cast down she saw a group of people walking along the middle of the street in a two-by-two formation. She squinted and her lenses zoomed in, showing the heavy weapons they carried. Even without the enhanced detail she would have made them for what they were.

"Yeah," she whispered, settling back in the shadows to wait. "That's the patrol from the 43rd Precinct. Their station's the next block over."

"Ballsy," Benji said, and Celeste could hear the grin in his voice as she imagined him looking down at the patrol from his perch above. "Not only did Clarion pick a place inside the Fence to keep this guy, but they did it within spitting distance of the local cops. I'm surprised they didn't just put him in Captain Nest's office."

"Or the general's bathroom," Celeste said, her lips curling.

"All right, that's enough," Aveen said, but smiling as he did. "That patrol will pass by here in another minute. Then we've got a short window of less than five to get all of you onto the roof of Yang's building before they come back. Celeste will take point, securing the entry on the roof. You two get over to her when she's got things ready. Any questions?"

"Yeah," Benji asked, his tone mock-thoughtful, "why aren't you coming? Don't leaders, I don't know, lead?"

"I forgot how funny you're not," Aveen said, shaking his head and not smiling. "I've got to stay down here and cover the entrance. It's the only one to the building, and if you geniuses screw up and trip an alarm, those cops will be coming up for a little heart to heart. I have to make sure they don't get through the door to add to the conversation."

"Do we have a confirmed number of hostiles inside?" Tofe asked, speaking up for the first time. His tone was serious, and Celeste frowned. Usually he was as relaxed as Benji.

"No," Aveen said. "But considering the value of the target, odds are he's got a few babysitters. Be ready for them."

The patrol lumbered along and while they waited for it to pass, Aveen took up his rifle and held it in a relaxed pose that could be quickly adjusted to lay down targeted fire, and she pulled on a pair of gloves and knee pads that emitted a faint blueish glow. When the six-man team turned the corner at the other end of the street Celeste motioned with her head to the top of the building across from them and pressed her fingers to her throat. "Proceeding to secure the entry point."

She checked her gloves and baseball-sized knee pads one last time, and after a running start across the empty street, she vaulted into the air and onto the corner of the building. Clapping her hands to either side of the 90-degree angle and following a half-second later with her knees, she dug her toes into the magnetic energy flowing just below the surface.

All buildings and the street she had just left were hidden rivers of magnetism. The power plants run by the Protectorate needed to be massive generators of it in order to maintain the Fence encircling the cities. The smaller portion of this output went into the homes and businesses of the empire, but it was still an amount sufficient to infuse all structures with invisible floods of power. The pads she wore took advantage of this, by providing an opposing charge. Her gloves, pads, and toes all pulled at the fields running inside and allowed her to use the wall itself for climbing, and was a favored means of accessing targets who otherwise thought themselves untouchable.

"Building the sandwich," as the action was nicknamed, involved pressing on the outside of the stone with the energy within pulling her gloves and pads toward it to form a strong seal. The building was the meat in the middle, and by cutting out the field in one knee, toe, or glove by a particular twist of wrist or hip, she could slide it up to reengage. The limbs on one side slid up the stone, reconnected, then the opposing side copied the action. Repeating the process saw her make her way up the building a few crawling feet at a time, and within a minute or two, she would reach the top and throw herself over the parapet to prepare the breach for her companions.

On top of the building that Aveen and Celeste had crouched beside were Tofe and Benji. They looked over the edge down at her as she ascended the corner of the apartment complex opposite them, and Benji pressed his finger to his throat as he stared with a sighing smile.

"Man, isn't Celeste just the best at climbing? Me, I've got too much muscle to get up the side of six stories."

Tofe rolled his eyes. "Yeah, real subtle. That's right up there with 'Hey attractive female, I need your sympathy. It's so hard carrying all this money around.' Or how about: 'Pardon me, can you help me figure out where to put this first place DOX Wars trophy? I've got several I need to put somewhere to make room for my citation for caring for widows and orphans.'"

Celeste grinned at the back and forth, pausing to take a breather of a few seconds by gripping the wall with toes and knees alone as she leaned back to shake out her burning forearms and biceps.

"Oh, don't worry, Ben," she said, as she pressed her neck, "you can use all that manly tissue to carry the target when we've extracted him. I'll even let you do it the whole way back to base."

"Sorry, darlin,'" Benji said, putting on a ridiculous cowboy accent, "I've got to see to the herd down at Oxbow Junction. Can't let m'self fall to dereliction of duty 'cause of a pretty face."

The commlink was filled with a sudden cacophony of groans. "God, you and your Western cinelinks," Tofe snorted. "You do realize horses went extinct a hundred years ago? You'd have a better chance of riding off into the sunset on a camel."

Celeste snickered at the idea of Benji trying to sweep her off her feet onto a testy two-humped dromedary as she resumed climbing. It was an open secret Benji had a crush on her and had ever since she had thrown him over her shoulder in their first grappling session at age 10.

"Wow," he had said that morning twelve years earlier, flat on his back on the pad of the combat training room, staring up at her with stars in his eyes. They came as much from her slamming him to the ground as the vision of loveliness she appeared as to him in that moment. She had thought he was simply faking his adoration and kept her hands at the ready to wrestle with him should he attempt a leg lock or to sweep her feet out from under her. But it was soon clear he was actually smitten with her, and this disarmed her more than any attack he might have tried.

In the years since, they had become close as friends, although everyone knew Benji hoped for more. For her part, Celeste only had eyes for Captain Nest's position as head instructor. She wanted to command, and saw Benji as a sweet, if foolish, distraction.

She shook the memory of him lying there with moony eyes and grin as she angled her left wrist at the side of the wall where the fourth and fifth floors met. The flat beam of golden light she cast onto the bare concrete in an up-and-down motion hummed, and she checked the results on her holographic display. "Scan of the eastern stairwell of the fourth floor's clear. I can't see any guards."

Aveen nodded. "Good. Easy in, easy out. Once she gives you the signal, get over there and the three of you work your way down to apartment 5E. I'm standing by to cover you at the base. If you need me to come up, I'll follow Celeste's track," he added, eyeing the angle of stonework she had scaled.

The group all acknowledged the command and the men kept talking as Celeste climbed. She paused outside the fifth floor and repeated her scan. She frowned as she considered the display. "Aveen? We've got a hefty presence on 5. I make out at least twenty bodies."

"Sentries or civilians?"

She cocked her head at the display, waving it slowly back and forth across the face of the stone in an attempt to improve the image's clarity. But as with the resolution of the Skip in the meeting room when Captain Nest reviewed their last run, the figures were without definition.

"Can't say. They're all in the hallway, with most lying down and a few standing. I can't see into the rooms themselves because of the partition walls."

"Are they armed?"

She shook her head. "If they have weapons they must be holstered on their hips. I can't see anyone holding something with two hands."

Aveen considered this and said that they had better skip the front door approach. "Fall back to a ceiling entry. The floors have identical layouts, so make your breach via apartment 6E."

Everyone confirmed the order and Celeste resumed climbing, her attention totally focused on the job at hand. A false grip or careless placement of her foot would see her plummet to the ground and crack like an underdone egg. But when Benji and Tofe's conversation drifted to the upcoming Assignation Ritual, she sucked in a breath.

"Come on, Tofe. You can't tell me it's never crossed your mind."

"I really don't think about it. Why should I, when I've got no control over it?"

A sigh. "Not the 'arranged marriage' shtick again."

"More like 'arranged miscarriage.'"

Benji snorted. "What are you talking about, man? The birthrate's 100%!"

"So what if it is? You'll never know your kid's name. You won't even know whether it's a boy or a girl. Pretty hard to call it your child when neither of you exist in the other's life."

Celeste's hand on the wall shook as she flattened her palm against the stone for another magnetic grip.

Such a stupid conversation. So utterly inane.

"Who'd want you as a dad, anyhow? You're about as cheery as a necrotic fungal infection."

Tofe couldn't stop himself from chuckling. "Yeah, because you're really focused on fatherhood. You're not looking forward to Assignation because there'll be a little 'you' running around."

"Hey, don't blame me for appreciating the process. Your problem is you're hung up on the product."

Celeste forced her hand to reach up, then her opposing knee, and set her toe against a seam in the concrete. She repeated the process with her other hand, knee, and foot, and did her best to ignore the conversation taking place a quarter-mile away on a rooftop. She wanted to tell them to shut up, but if she did Benji would just rib her for cutting in. And it was no good appealing to Aveen for radio silence. He let such chatter continue up until it was time to breach, claiming it helped ease tension.

All the more reason to get to the top as fast as possible.

They would all be selected, she knew. Assignation was a requirement for all agents. But the thought of being a mother sent a thrill of terror through her. It was mixed with hot shame at knowing she would neither hold nor ever see her child. But the idea some part of her would go on, would be independent of her knowledge or wishes, was something warm and comforting. It offset the taking of life she so often did. But the possibility—the near-certainty—her child would be scaling walls like the one she was climbing in order to infiltrate a target's sanctuary made her hands tremble once more.

That she was one such result was a private pain she sought never to dwell on. Whereas almost all of the agents were children whose families donated them to the cause or were simply orphans who the Protectorate adopted for their special forces, some Cicadas were the product of the annual Assignation. Celeste suspected the youngest group of present Cicadas were made up entirely of the forced coupling of agents, and she would be expected to be amongst the next generation of carriers. One of the eggs taken from her before puberty would be reimplanted, and a randomly assigned male agent would impregnate her, the act neither consensual, nor she suspected, particularly sensual.

She felt sick as she reached the top of the wall and threw herself over the parapet. She crouched there for half a minute with her back to the three-foot-high brick guard wall. This shielded her from Benji and Tofe's line of sight and helped slow her breathing as she tried to force her attention back to the mission. As she did she felt a tingling on the right side of her chest. She blinked at the unfamiliar feeling and reached inside the pocket of her tactical vest where a small buzzing note emanated. She blinked and frowned, then removed the multicolored card the stranger had given her at the bar.

She had kept it with her even though it seemed a useless gesture. Her scans of it when returning from her exam revealed nothing, and as it was not poisoned nor was it a pocket-sized EMP bomb, she just forgot about it. But now it was pulsing with soft colored light, and she squinted at it. Suddenly it flashed in her hand and she dropped it to the concrete of the rooftop where it lay. Before she could radio to the others about it, a stream of nanites poured up to coalesce into the figure of a person. After a few seconds, the man who had given her the disguised memdisk card stood before her, a one-foot-high hologram.

10

THE DEAD RISE

"*H*ello," he said with the same charming smile he offered her at the ball. "My name is... well, my name isn't important at the moment. I used to be called Glider, although I don't go by it anymore. You might've heard of me, then again you might not have. It doesn't really matter. It is enough that I'm coming to you in this way to make you realize that my intentions involve you. This recording cannot be replayed and was triggered when you neared one of the DOX portal safehouses. Which one doesn't matter. General Aepal sent you here, and that can only be to hurt someone innocent inside of it."

Celeste's heart rate spiked when he said the name Glider. This was the most famous agent of the entire service, and all the more so because of the mystery of his disappearance. It happened more than a decade earlier and had something to do with him vanishing into the DOX with a *mencist* whose name she couldn't recall. So if he really was who was talking to her now, that was shocking in itself. But what he went on to say collapsed her world.

"I do not for a moment assume that you trust everything—or really anything—I have to say," the digital figure said, inclining his head in concession, "but it will be obvious to even the most dedicated Agent that there are problems with the Protectorate. I should know, because I used to be one of you."

As Celeste leaned closer to better hear, her ear beeped to announce a transmission.

"We're ready over here," Benji whispered. "The stairs and floor below clear?"

Her fingers fumbled at her throat and she replied: "One second. I'm still scanning for hostiles."

The pre-recorded message continued while she responded to her teammate, and she felt frustration at having lost several seconds of what the man was saying. Her focus once more on him, she devoured his words in mid-sentence as she tried to fill in the gaps in context.

"...will all make sense in the end. For now, I need you to believe that you are not my enemy. None of the agents are really opposed to Clarion in purpose. And while yes, it is easy for you to believe I am simply trying to turn you to our cause, you have seen what you have seen, and you have done what you've done. You know that the system is broken. And it is the Protectorate which broke it. You helped do it. I helped do it."

"In the coming days," he went on, looking up at her with calm, almost sad eyes, "there will come a reckoning. It is no secret that General Aepal plans to invade the DOX looking to claim what he says is a doomsday weapon. This is not at all what he's looking for. But since I cannot be certain of your ultimate involvement or whether or not you can see the truth, I cannot provide any more details in this message. But someone who could give you a better sense of my past and whether to trust me is Aveen."

"Aveen?" Celeste whispered, confused.

"Like all of us, he was lied to all of his life. The core of it is that Romania isn't all that's left. There is a whole world beyond the Fence."

Celeste's stomach clenched. "That's a lie. There's nothing beyond the Fence but the DOX! Nothing but the dragging dead!"

The recording seemed to have guessed her response. "The DOX isn't the end of things, it is the beginning. The Earth isn't some fragile piece of paper that will tear every time humans do something stupid. There are whole other life forms out here that show what I mean. Whole other worlds that the Protectorate doesn't want you to see."

Now her stomach dropped and she whispered softly, "What?"

"The Protectorate is just a fishbowl within the wider world. When you're sent out to search for the 'weapon,'" he emphasized his dismissal of the concept with a droll expression, "we will make contact with you. We will show you the truth if you let us. Aepal has tried to conceal it for your entire life, but his walls are breaking down. It's just about the only thing the Protectorate and we agree on: truth rises."

"As for Aveen," Glider said, "he's how you can find me out here. He might still hate me for leaving without telling him the secret he was always pestering me for. But ask him about it, and he'll know it's really me and not some Skip pretending. You can say—"

"The patrol will make their next pass in one minute," Aveen said in her ear, nearly stopping her heart and breaking her attention on the recording. "Tofe and Benji take off immediately."

"Shit!" She hissed and whipped out a small flashlight with a green lens from a pocket on her vest. She turned back to the nanite figure in time to catch him say: "... and so that's how you'll find me. The answer to his question will lead him to me."

"Goddamn it, what question?" she hissed, twisting the shaft of the light to power it on.

"But be assured," he said, as his nanite form began to dissolve, "we know that you are coming. That should be enough to tell you such an incursion is at the least ill-advised, and at worst a suicide mission. But I will leave you with the promise that we are not enemies. We don't want to kill you. And we don't want you to kill any more innocent people, as you know you have done. As I told you: it's important to know that you're hurting the right people. Aren't you tired of the Protectorate hurting you, and telling you it's right?"

As the haze of the nanites dispersed on the wind and the card grew dark, Celeste sat there trembling. What she had heard shook her to her very core, and made her question everything that had brought her to the rooftop. Her birth, the brutal training since infancy, the disappearance of people who had questioned the Protectorate's methods, and most recently the two cadets who general Aepal had executed right in front of their peers.

It could very well be a high-level PSYOP on the part of Clarion, as the figure claiming to be the vanished agent openly admitted. It would not be the first time that such devious tactics were employed in war. She had carried out some of her own. But Celeste had the feeling the man was being so open with her because he truly did have more knowledge than she did. Whether it would help protect the citizens of the nation, as the agents were charged to do, was another question. And whether she wanted to hear the information that might unravel her whole world in the process was another.

Aveen's harsh whisper sliced into her right ear. "Agent! I can see the patrol at the end of the street! Is the roof secure?"

Celeste winced and pressed her fingers to her throat as she stared at the now-useless piece of plastic lying on the concrete before her. "Affirmative. Ready to receive extraction team." And she began clicking the flashlight at the rooftop where her companions would arrive from.

Benji heard the exchange between the team leader and his colleague, and frowned.

That's not like Celeste. She'll say something funny or cutting, but she's always on the ball. What's going on over there?

He did not have time to ask over the radio or even to bring up the subject with Tofe. The man next to him was already standing and throwing out his arms with a snapping emotion that extended a pair of metal mesh membranes between the wrists and ankles of his LT suit. Benji jumped to his feet and did likewise, and without another word, the pair of them leapt off the rooftop with their faces pointed toward where the bright green flash of light repeated on the rooftop across the street. It was the handheld laser strobe Celeste held to guide them in, and the wind washed over Benji and whistled in his ears as he flattened himself on the breeze with his eyes locked onto it.

He saw Tofe gliding farther ahead of him and he swore. *Damn it. I should have gotten a running start.*

Tofe drifted ahead of him with a perfect posture, a swimmer through the night using the space between the buildings as his lane. Benji followed in his wake and had to resort to a "dolphin kick" to maintain his altitude. The technique was meant to help a flier muscle through a headwind, but Benji needed to gyrate his legs and hips in a noodling motion just to stay aloft. He looked down and saw the small knot of soldiers crawling along the center of the street and kicked harder.

I'll be a lovely target up here for them if they see me.

The noodling motion was ugly but it worked. He closed the distance to the opposite rooftop and at the last second propelled himself up and over the parapet by bringing both hands down in a tremendous clap. This vaulted him over the low wall of stone to land on his feet in a crouch beside Tofe.

"Real slick move," Tofe said, grinning at him as his heart hammered in his chest. "I thought Aveen was going to have to scrape you off the sidewalk."

"Hey," Benji said, his grin wide as he placed his feet together and pressed his hands to his sides as Tofe was doing to cause their suits to pull the flight membranes into the seams running from armpit to ankle, "it takes a lot of skill to look this good. Don't hate because you can't manage to—"

"What the hell was that?" Aveen hissed over the comm. "I heard it down here!"

So apparently did the patrol. Aveen synced his lenses to theirs so they could see the half-dozen heavily-armed troops pause in front of the double steel doors of the apartment building. He squinted to zoom in and the three on the roof had to resist the urge to look over the edge down at the men looking up.

Benji hated syncing. Some loved it; he didn't. It overlaid what the wearer was seeing onto the view of those he was connected to. "Ghosting" a person usually meant to skip out of meeting them or otherwise leave them waiting for you without giving them notice. In the agent community, it was when the view of one team member allowed the others to see what he saw, without completely obscuring their own vision.

"Damn it!" Celeste hissed as the city soldiers walked over to inspect the entrance of their building. On the roof where they crouched this appeared as a group of pale holograms passing among her and Benji and Tofe. One of the ghostly soldiers remained in the street with his rifle held across his body, staring up at the dark sky and turning in a slow circle.

As his perspective played out for them on the roof, Aveen considered aborting the mission. They couldn't fight them; first, as they weren't equipped with the body armor and heavy weapons the city patrol carried. Odds are he could take down two or at most three of them before they figured out where the shots were coming from and rushed his position. The second reason was agents were among the Protectorate's deniable assets. If he didn't kill all of them and was captured, no one would be coming to rescue them.

"When you exist, you can be caught. But if you don't, no one looks for you. Agents don't exist," General Aepal told the cadets when they turned 14 and began going into the field for limited missions. "If any of you pop up on the nightly vidstream, you will get no help from us. You get yourself into trouble, you get out. And if you try to pull this program into it, you'll get our attention all right. For as long as it takes to put a bullet in you."

But just as he chambered a round and put the scope on the forehead of the first soldier, their leader signaled them to walk away from the front of the building. He couldn't hear the order over the distance, but they were obviously uninterested in further inquiry into Benji's last-minute landing sound. The man in the street staring upward went last, having been called away from continuing to survey the rooftops. As they left, and Aveen let out a sigh.

"Glad to see we didn't have to get carted off to the local lockup," he muttered into his throat, as he flicked the safety back onto his rifle and disengaged the sync. "But a few months in a Corp prison will be Christmas morning compared to what I'll do to you if you fuck up again," he growled, his gaze traveling up the side of the building across the street.

Tofe chuckled as he and the others reached over their shoulders to pull their Scorpion rifles around. "Don't blame him, Cap'n," he said, shaking his head at Benji who felt simultaneously sick to his stomach and hot in the face with shame. "Big Ben can't help his lack of aerodynamics. All that muscle he's carrying around wasn't meant to soar."

"Cut the chatter and go get the target," Aveen said, watching the patrol reach the end of the block and disappear around the corner. "You've got ten minutes until they circle back."

Tofe acknowledged the order with a smile, then turning serious, took his fingers from his throat and looked at Celeste.

"What's going on? You're not okay, so don't bother saying you are."

She caught him staring at her, his face concerned. She opened her mouth to speak but Benji brought his rifle across his body to cradle it with both hands. "I'll take 12. You two cover 3-6-9."

Celeste nodded and moved to follow Benji toward the steel door built into the sloping side of the roof's access staircase. Tofe watched them go, his eyes narrowing. But with the clock ticking he said nothing and fell in line behind her. She took a position sweeping a 45-degree angle to the left and back to make sure no one hit them from behind with Tofe doing the same for the right 45 degrees.

She's supposed to take point and Ben the rear, Tofe thought, feeling discomfort about what was supposed to be a straightforward operation. He looked at the pair approaching the door and shook his head, trying to keep his focus on his suddenly altered part of the team. *Ben wants to make up for muffing the landing, and something's screwing with Celeste's head.*

The door presented no difficulty, and they breached it by frying the electronic lock and slipping inside, all three not speaking as they went.

"Did you pick up any hostiles on the sixth floor?" Tofe murmured from the rear as they lightly padded down the stairs to the interior door leading to the hallway. Celeste didn't respond at first and when they reached the metal door Benji turned back to her, an eyebrow raised.

She looked at a spot just to the right of his face and said nothing. Tofe frowned and was about to say something when Aveen's voice whispered in their right ears. "Status? Have you located Dr. Guozhi yet?"

No one answered as both men eyed Celeste. She swallowed and they frowned at her.

Jesus, Tofe thought. *Did she not scan the floors? What the hell happened to her?*

Instead of asking this out loud, Tofe raised his fingertips to his throat. "Took a little longer to clear the floor, Cap'n. We're going in now."

11

HEARTH AND HOME

*T*he sixth floor was deserted when Benji pushed open the door. The red carpet running the length of the hallway between the rooms was faded and threadbare, and the lights overhead looked 30 years out of date.

Benji almost made a joke about the peeling paint to ease the tension but kept his mouth closed. He led them along the hallway and tried to avoid stepping anywhere that creaked, but it wasn't possible to predict every sigh and groan of the old wood beneath them. But they reached the end of the hall without any apartment doors opening, and Benji let out a soft breath of relief and angled the barrel of his rifle downward as they gathered outside of the door to 6E.

Ready? He mouthed to the others.

They nodded, and just as Benji was about to overload the maglock, Tofe grabbed his wrist and whispered: "Remember, incapacitation rounds only."

"Yes," Celeste said, her voice flat. "We don't want to hurt the wrong people."

Benji looked from one to the other, not liking either's mood. Tofe was acting like the squad captain when Celeste should have been, and she was acting as though hit by some terrible news on the roof. The only thing he had noticed after his disastrous landing was a memdisk put into card form lying at her feet. Which meant all of nothing. It was just one piece of trash amongst many cans and bottles, and couldn't have accounted for her out-of-character acting now.

But they had a job to do, and the longer it took to do it the more likely they would have to deal with the patrol outside or something worse inside. So without comment, he flicked the safety off of his Scorpion and selected it to fire non-lethal ammunition.

Celeste stepped up to the rectangular panel beside the solid-core door and placed her right wrist over it. She typed commands and the gauntlet began siphoning energy from the walls into it. The lights in the ceiling overhead flickered several times, and when a small light just below her thumb turned green, she looked away. The panel crackled with the sudden rush of electricity being poured into it, and its own red light beside the fingerprint reader went dark.

The door clicked open, and Celeste withdrew her hand from the panel, gripping her rifle. All three of them rushed inside the door and slid it closed. It couldn't fully engage as the current connecting it to the wall was cut. But it wasn't likely to be noticed by anyone walking down the hallway. The apartment residents were another matter, but they were home and asleep.

Tofe let his rifle hang from its strap attached to his vest and raised his left wrist as they spent a few seconds adjusting to the near-total darkness of the entryway and living room. It wasn't their eyes but the lenses affixed to them that needed the moment, and as the room slowly built in lime-tinted definition, he typed a few keys that appeared as a hologram over the back of his arm.

The command entered, the same fan of green laser light played over the living room they stood in as had emerged from Celeste's gauntlet when she climbed the side of the building. This synced to their lenses and the seismographic and thermal images over-layed the furnishings of the small space in lacy patterns of shining green.

"I'll take the mother and father," Tofe whispered to them as the horizontal shapes of two people appeared on the far wall, indi-cating they lay in the next room, "and you handle the kids. Meet back here ASAP."

He turned away before either she or Benji could say anything, and she seemed grateful for the order. Benji was irritated. Tofe was his best friend and a month younger, but was acting like he and Celeste were the lowest-ranking team members. But as she turned away to slip into the bedroom on the right end of the hall-way, sliding the dial on her Scorpion to the pale blue end where non-lethal rounds would be called from, he sighed and turned toward the left.

It was all an act, Tofe knew, as he struggled to appear decisive and unemotional. Whatever happened to Celeste on the roof wasn't good, and had already compromised the mission. He didn't want to lead, but he felt he had no choice. Benji might let his feelings for her get the better of him and issue orders that he thought spared her stress. But coddling her would probably get them all killed. Either from whoever had guns on the floor below where the scientist was being held, or from General Aepal himself if they returned without the target.

Tofe stood in the darkness of the bedroom listening to the soft snoring of the couple, his thoughts far away.

The general would already have killed me if he knew I let them go. I can't afford to slip up now despite whatever's scrambled Celeste's brains.

The people on the bed slept on while the assassin stood over them, his rifle pointed down at their exposed necks. The lake and the family fishing from his final exam came back to him as he stood there, and the question of whether he had done the right thing pushed its way onto the covers to lie beside the sleeping man and women.

Tofe had walked forward with his rifle held in a firing position on the back of the man's head. When he was ten feet away the daughter saw him and screamed. This sent the entire Kaufman family into the postures of terrified deer: frozen and wide-eyed.

He ordered the man to face him and he considered his trembling features as the red laser sight rested over the bridge of the man's nose. His arms were raised over his head and the children began to sniffle, then weep.

After half a minute he lowered the gun. "You are dead, understand? I shot you and your family 90 seconds ago and came forward to ensure there's nothing left. And there's not, correct?"

Kaufman blinked and slowly lowered his arms. He nodded. "Y-yes. We're all gone. We, um, we can go to—"

"Don't tell me," Tofe said, holding up a hand. "And don't tell anyone. Don't stay with anyone you know. Get fresh IDs and start over somewhere else."

"Now wait just a damn minute," the woman began to say, surging forward. Her husband caught her and pulled her back, but she kept talking, her words pouring out with increasing rage. "You're one of those goddamn agents, aren't you? The ones who go around killing anyone who complains about the government!"

Tofe stared her down. "I was. And your husband must have done something to piss off the Protectorate. I suggest you take your kids somewhere else and talk over what that was. Unless you prefer I carry out my original assignment?"

She opened her mouth to argue but her husband clapped a hand over it. "No, no we're good. We're grateful. And we're leaving. Come on, kids."

He half-carried her a few steps before she shook him loose. Her son and daughter ran to them both, with the boy going to the mother while the girl hugged the father. Tofe watched them collect themselves, and as they started walking off the father turned back.

"Why did you do this?"

Tofe stared down at the sleeping man and woman, the memory of Kaufman's concerned face on that of the man as though synced. "Children shouldn't have to watch their parents die."

As Kaufman and his wife watched him reverse his rifle so that the butt of it pointed at him.

"What are you doing?" she asked.

Tofe sighed. "Keeping them from thinking I just let you go."

And he swung the gun up to crack against the side of his head. The woman gave a little scream and Kaufman looked shocked, and the girl turned the boy's face away.

Tofe reached up through the haze of pain and dizziness and touched the dribble of blood that started its slide down his face. "It's enough," he said, his vision swimming. "You go on, now."

$\sim$

He whispered the same thing to the dark bedroom, then shot each of the people laying in the bed before him in the neck with an IncapaciPatch. They struggled in sudden wakefulness before falling back into deep sleep. Tofe stood over them for another few seconds, his fingers tracing the scar Dr. Nelson had left from the procedure to ease the swelling, and then turned to step into the hallway.

When Benji stepped into the room, he was struck by how many things were in it. A tall bookcase stood by the door on his right, while an even larger one was against the left sidewall.

God, he thought as he peered at it, *that thing's got enough stuffed animals to open a store.*

Between the toys scattered all over the floor and the pictures plastered onto every wall, the bedroom looked as though a child's birthday party had exploded.

But it was the turning figure of a ballerina on the nightstand which took his breath. Seeing the tiny figure of a woman on her toes with arms rainbowed over her and fingers clasped made his heart lurch, and he walked forward to stand beside the bed. By the glow of the little nanite night light he could see a dark-haired little girl with the covers pulled to her chin and a faint smile on her face.

The pale, feminine colors of the lamp played over the girl's features as the woman turned in place on her black disk, and Benji felt his stomach clench as he looked between the two, and the memory of the last time he saw such a dancer forced its way into his mind.

~

"For the last time I'm telling you, I don't have any connection to Clarion!"

The old woman stood hunched in a corner of the hotel's store-room, her cheeks wet with angry tears. Her purple shawl had come loose and fallen to the floor, and her fists were balled. Her left hand still held the *memdisk* of a young girl dancing.

"I wouldn't be here if you were just some sweet old lady meeting her girlfriends for lunch," Benji shot back, the syringe in his own left hand and thumb on the plunger. "And you wouldn't be much of a collaborator if you looked like a terrorist!"

He had approached her ten minutes earlier saying that he was sent to repair a faulty door lock on her room, and she was at first confused. She had not asked for help, she said. But she agreed to accompany him to the room to check on it. Once they were out of the lobby and in a side passage he suddenly opened a store-room and shoved her inside.

The following minutes consisted of him accusing her of spreading *dreamscape* and poisoning the citizens of the Protec-torate. But instead of pleading for her life or weeping and professing her innocence, she was angry.

"I don't give a hoot what you say I've done, I know the truth! I'm no plague peddler, and I'm not connected to Clarion no way, shape, or form! You've either got a screwloose or you're one of those godless agents who go running around killing innocent people!"

He knew it was the type of denial an operative deeply embedded would say. PSYOPs had taught them that when confronted with their own treachery, Clarion members could present with all manner of responses. Typically this meant a pulse pistol or elec-tric knife. But an old woman wouldn't attempt such physical attacks. She would use her words, her tears, and do precisely what this one was trying.

Benji didn't know why he hadn't just jabbed her in the neck and hurled her into the storeroom. Why did he talk to her? Give her the chance to use her forked tongue on him?

She suddenly stood up straighter. Her face took on a defiant expression and her chin lifted. "I've lived 69 years on this Earth. I've buried a husband and two children to *dreamscape*, and I haven't hurt no one that didn't deserve it. So if you want to come and kill me, then go ahead. I'm going to take a chunk out of your ass on the way out, though."

She put up her fists and glared at him, and for a moment Benji didn't know what to do. Then he thought of the tiny girl turning on the old woman's memdisk, and he sighed.

"You have to disappear now. Either because I kill you and burn the body in the hotel's furnace, or you go somewhere no one knows you. The choice is yours, and it needs to happen in the next 30 seconds."

Benji stared at the small, slowly-turning ballerina beside the little girl's bed, and let out a breath with a smile. "She chose to go," he whispered, looking from the nanite dancer to the child's face. "I just hope she was your grandmother." His face stretched in a wide smile. "I wish she was mine."

After slipping inside the right-hand bedroom Celeste walked up to the side of the single bed. She raised the rifle and was about to pull the trigger when her eyes landed on a small colorful book on the nightstand. She blinked at it and looked at the girl. The child was perhaps 10, and her honey-blonde hair wrapped around her face in a frame that gave Celeste pause. She was asleep and wouldn't wake until the dime-sized chemical patch hit her below her left ear.

The man on the roof—Glider—came to her as she looked at the child. Was she hurting someone who didn't deserve it? The answer was yes. Simply that, with no possibility to contest it.

We broke into these people's home only to go through the floor for the apartment below. They did nothing to deserve it, and there will be no payment by the program to cover their loss. They will never admit we were here.

She stepped to the nightstand and took up the book. It was a diary and the lock on the cover was open. Celeste opened the slim pink volume and found an inscription.

> *To Jamie. May all your sweetest secrets be kept here, so you'll never lose them! Love, Mom and Dad.*

Celeste hesitated, then turned to the first page.

> *February 7, 2303. I have my first diary! So cool! I will put all my best thoughts into it. My brightest ideas and my fears too. Daddy says it's important to accept things that make you afraid. It makes you stronger!*

Celeste found her eyes wet as she flipped through the pages. And when she reached June she froze.

> *June 3, 2303. Mommy and Daddy are so tired these days. I hope they're not sick. They just sleep all the time. They talk to things I can't see—*

"Shit!" Celeste hissed, backing out of the room with the diary still in her hand. On the threshold, she stopped and hurried forward to the bedside once more. She raised the rifle and shot the girl in the neck. The child's eyes fluttered open, and she looked up to lock them with Celeste. Then the lids slid closed and she returned to sleep. Celeste watched her for a moment before tearing herself away and out of the room.

"Evac!" she hissed into her throat as she moved down the hallway toward the living room. "They're Dreamers!"

12

GRATITUDE OF THE DAMNED

*T*he alert hit the others' ears like a gunshot. Aveen down in the shadow of the two buildings started at it, and his spasm caused him to grip the stock of the rifle in a sudden jerk as though it had shocked him. "Report!" he hissed, after recovering. "What were the symptoms? Are they attacking you?"

Celeste, Tofe, and Benji met in the living room, one hand on their respective guns and the other pressed to their throats. Tofe spoke first. "I saw no indications of it with the two adults I just tranqed. Ben?"

He shook his head. "Nothing I caught. I wasn't looking all that closely, though. It was just a sleeping girl in a bed. It's after midnight, so that's normal."

They both looked at Celeste, and for a moment she felt a stab of doubt as she held up the book. "It was something the kid in my room wrote. She put in her diary that her parents were sleeping a lot and were talking to things she couldn't see."

Aveen considered this. It didn't sound like the traditional presentation of people lost in an alternate reality, but it was well known the virus mutated. It might simply look different for these people. And conversing with the invisible was certainly common.

"Was there any bruising under the eyes?" he asked. "Any blood around the irises?"

"None that I saw," Tofe replied.

Benji agreed. "Her eyes opened pretty wide when I hit her with the tranquilizer. But with about a second to look—and my not looking for streaks from the engorged veins—I can't say for sure."

Aveen didn't want to second guess his lieutenant, especially in the middle of a run. She had inexplicably acted odd on the roof already, and he didn't want to tip her into something worse by getting after her now.

"All right, just breach the floor and grab the mark. We'll have to quarantine when we get back to base regardless. In the meantime, everyone take an extra jab of ramps."

The three acknowledged the command after bringing their hands to their necks. Then each pulled a small vial containing a pale blue liquid and opened their mouths, with Celeste slipping the diary into an inside pocket next to the empty memdisk.

"Man, I hate this stuff," Benji said, groaning as he cracked the seal and sucked the contents down. His face twisted. "Tastes like a blueberry's butthole."

Tofe shrugged as his vial of immune system boosters went down. "Beats the alternative. Knowing my luck, I'd just get dreams of you trying to flex on Celeste. Talk about a nightmare."

She grimaced as she swallowed her dose. "Almost as bad as if I had to dream about you two arguing who was the better DOX Champion. That would be a fate worse than death."

Benji slipped his empty vial into his thigh pocket and grinned. "That's pointless. Everyone knows Voss the Ravager's the all-time best. He's won more titles than anyone!"

"Sure," Tofe snorted, pocketing his own vial, "and that has nothing to do with being President Cesque's nephew. Nope. Not a thing."

The tension somewhat diffused, although no one truly felt in a joking mood, nothing more was said. They set to work on the floor in the living room, each carrying out a portion of the job. Celeste scanned the apartment and hallway below to check for load-bearing beams or sentries on patrol. Benji removed a coil of translucent wire the width of a pencil and placed it in a circle on the floor where Celeste pointed. It stuck there in a five-foot ring, and he attached a small lead wire to it, then connected the wire to his left wrist.

As Tofe magnetically adhered a trio of slender ropes to the ceiling above where Benji laid the breaching cable, Benji grinned up at him. "Hey, did you know that this whole area used to be a market?"

"A what?" Celeste asked as she peered at the scan floating above her right wrist. The human shapes she saw earlier were still in the hallway below them, and they weren't moving. Three figures were in the apartment, however, and she tried to make out if any were carrying weapons. But the featureless silhouettes didn't seem to be pacing in any regular pattern as guards would have. One paused at what looked like a table, and the other two carried something back and forth or wrote something on a clipboard.

She was about to say that the room below was clear of armed personnel when Benji continued. "A market, the largest in Bucharest for over 1,000 years. It was a major stopping point on the Silk Road. People from China in the east, all the way to Prague and even Switzerland on the western end."

"The road was made out of silk?" Tofe asked, giving each line a quick pull to ensure it was securely attached.

Benji looked up at him, his face disturbed. "Oh. That was a serious question." He sighed and shook his head. "You guys give me shit for watching old movies, but you ingrates don't do anything to improve yourselves. Hell, you don't even know the basic history of the country you're defending!"

Tofe released the ropes and picked up his Scorpion from where he had laid it to rest against the couch. "Yeah, spending all our time fighting people trying to turn the place into a biological wasteland is no excuse. How uncultured we all are!"

"If we show up at someone's door, odds are they did something to bring us there," Celeste murmured, no trace of humor in her voice as she stared straight ahead and spoke the catchphrase Cicadas learned from their earliest days. Her thoughts were on what Glider had said. That, and the countless people she had hurt or killed since she went on her first mission at 14. The memories were not accompanied by the usual feeling of calm satisfaction in knowing she had saved innocent civilians. Now the images of their faces as she pulled the trigger, pushed their heads under-water to soften them up for interrogation, or tortured them herself, came bringing something else entirely. The feeling was hard, cold, and heavy. It sat like a sharp-edged block of ice in her stomach. With an effort, she pushed it away. Compartmentalized it as she had been taught.

No more was said as they magnetically attached the ropes to the back of their LT suits. They hefted their rifles and looked at each other. All nodded and stepped inside the circle. Benji tapped the pale red button floating over his left wrist. The coil on the floor began to glow and then to hum. When the soles of their feet began to vibrate each tensed.

The detonation was powerful but muted. The reinforced side of the plastic tube caught the omnidirectional blast of plasma and sent it back toward the side adhered to the floor. This flash-burned the tile and the wood beneath it, and a second after it began, the chemical chain reaction sliced through the ceiling of the floor beneath them.

It crumbled and they fell through, the drop arrested by the cables locked to their backs. Within three seconds of pressing the red button, the trio landed hard on the floor of apartment 5E's living room. This would have broken the ankles of most people, but their LT suits absorbed and redirected the kinetic energy of what amounted to their landing with the force of two tons. This rippled the air around them and puffed out the clouds of fine particles from the breach, and the waves of it cleared the air in a twenty-foot bubble.

They immediately stood back-to-back as the smoke of settling plaster and burned wood and tile swirled outward from them. This revealed the living room of the apartment had been converted into a laboratory, and numerous microscopes, flasks and beakers, and a chemical hood built into the back wall were visible, as well as many banks of computers and drive towers.

From each point of their triangle, the agents covered one of the three people in the room with their rifles. "Which one of you is Dr. Jieshi Yang?" Tofe snapped, the red light of his gun's laser square in the center of the older woman's chest five feet in front of him. Her hands held a clipboard and her eyes were wide, but she said nothing. Like the other two, she wore a white lab coat and looked exhausted.

After a moment her expression changed, and she looked at him with cold hostility. "You are the Protectorate's assassins."

"We're not here for violence," Tofe replied, tightening the grip on his weapon. "Give us Dr. Yang and we all go home to our families."

The woman's lips peeled back in rage, but her voice only frosted. "Go back to them? How? Move into the cemetery where you put them?"

The three blinked at the accusation, their eyes faltering on their respective targets.

The woman glared at Tofe, the veins in her neck distorted by anger as she spat accusations at him. "Two years ago, you took my son and husband from me. Shot them down in the middle of a park. Blew a pair of holes in them and afterwards called them terrorist collaborators. Slapped the label of it right over the bullet holes like it was a band-aid for society."

"Look, lady," Tofe began, "I have no idea what you're talking about. But we're not here to hurt anyone. If your family was shot in some raid of a Clarion nest—"

"They were in the goddamn park!" she screamed, hurling her clipboard from her. "In the open! Unarmed and not bothering anyone!"

Tofe felt his insides clench in the face of her fury, but before he could try to diffuse the situation Benji called out: "I've got him."

Tofe spared a look to where Benji was holding his gun on a gray-headed Asian man, and in that moment the old woman reached into a dark green plastic toolbox on the metal examination table beside her. Tofe caught the motion out of the corner of his eye and snapped his head back around. Only his training got his shot off first, and the Bulldog round slammed into the woman's chest and hurled her backwards over the table. It was a solid rubber ball the size of a quarter and the crack of ribs sounded loud in the small space. Her gun went with her, disappearing out of sight, and Tofe gave her a few seconds to rise and try again. But there was silence.

Celeste's man held his hands up higher, and his voice rose to a corresponding pitch. "Please! Don't hurt us!"

"Then don't give us a reason to," Benji snapped, his eyes on the Asian man. "That was a non-lethal round. Don't force us to switch to something more lasting."

As the man burbled he wasn't resisting, Benji considered who they had come for. Dr. Yang was considerably thinner than the image they saw floating above their wrists before the run started, and had a three-day growth of beard and his eyes were bloodshot in the light of the floor lamps scattered along the edges of the room. All consistent with a man kept hostage for a long period. But he was looking with fixed intensity at the intruders in a way that didn't suggest joy at his departure.

Rules out Dreaming, Benji thought, squinting to zoom in on the man's eyes. *That means he's here with us and not off in crazyland. But he sure doesn't look happy.*

"We're here to rescue you," he said, deciding Yang might be thinking they were there to kill him because of his expression. But the old man shook his head with a look of tired disgust.

"No, you're here to take me to prison. Or kill me. Aepal sent you, or one of his cronies in the World Security Council. And it wasn't to rescue me."

His words stabbed Celeste, and she took her eyes off of her target to look at the old man. "Why do you say that? What are you doing for Clarion?"

He looked from Benji to her, his expression dark and wary. "Of course you wouldn't know what we're doing here. To you, everyone outside the Fence is a terrorist. Everyone who thinks for themselves is a threat. You're a bullet. And a bullet doesn't know why its being fired."

Wincing at the coming feeling of nausea the experience always brought him, Benji synced his lenses and locked his gaze on the man before him. Their rescuee wasn't acting at all like he should, and the night had already gone sideways with Celeste's unexplained actions on the roof. Aveen needed to see what was happening for himself and tell them what to do.

Down on the street, their leader blinked at suddenly seeing their target standing before him in a gauze of pale green light. He was about to press his fingers to his throat and ask what the hell was going on, when he froze at what the holographic ghost said.

"You think I'm helping them create a new *dreamscape*, don't you? Something to gas the people within the Fence with and turn them all into a slobbering mass of tearing flesh and wild-eyed insanity?"

Celeste brought her gaze back to the man she was supposed to be covering with her rifle. With the lenses synced she could still see Yang's expressions, and she spoke to the glimmering green figure overlaying the man before her as though speaking with their target.

"You were kidnapped from a Protectorate lab a year ago. That wouldn't happen if you wanted to go willingly. And Clarion wouldn't be holding you in this building crawling with Dreamers you could experiment on to make a new line of men's cologne."

He sighed and shook his head. "Your tongue might be sharp but your wits are dull. You were lied to, and don't have the intelligence to question it. This building did have many suffering from the virus, yes. Clarion used it as a safehouse of sorts; put many here so they couldn't infect others. But also so that they could be treated. And 'treated' is the key word, agent. The Protectorate treats Dreamers as something to be stopped, not saved."

His words stung Tofe, as they pushed the memory of his parents into his mind. He gritted his teeth and kept his eyes on the over-turned table. The old woman wasn't moving based on the foot around the edge of the table he could see, but he kept his gun trained on the metal rectangle.

He cleared his throat and said: "So you really expect us to believe Clarion's the hero and the Protectorate is the villain, huh? That old tired line of propaganda?"

Dr. Yang sighed. "You just shot a woman whose family was murdered by your colleagues. I don't expect to change your mind about anything."

"So you're not here against your will?" Celeste asked, her voice tight.

"No. Does that mean you will shoot me like you did Dr. Carter? Or her family?"

"Damn it, that wasn't us!" Tofe snapped.

"So what *are* you doing here?" Benji asked, not liking the emotion coming from both of his teammates. "Our intel suggests you've been developing an updated version of the *dreamscape* virus. And here we find you in a Clarion-controlled building cooking with something in the middle of the night, and one of your group just tried to kill us after accusing us of murdering her family. You can imagine why it's more than a little hard to believe you're just misunderstood victims."

Dr. Yang gave a little shrug, the gesture a concession. "Fair enough. But it doesn't change the reality. I wasn't brought here to build a better virus, nor use the sufferers of the first one to concoct a stronger version. I was doing it to cure them. And I have. It was the least I could do, considering what Nelson and I created."

Every eye widened at this and Aveen hissed into his comm. "Cure? Nelson? What the hell is this guy talking about?"

Tofe watched the old man for several seconds, then let out a tired breath.

"He's Dr. Guozhi Jiang. A dead man come to life, and bringing a cure with him."

13

BLOOD AND FLOWERS

"*B*ut-but those people in the hallway," Celeste began, her heart clenching along with the rest of the team in the room and on the street. "The family in the apartment above—"

"Ah, yes," the man claiming to be Dr. Jiang said, nodding, "the Muellers. The parents were infected, it is true. They were very close to madness when they were brought to me. But Clarion cared for their children while I worked on the moAbs, and after a week they woke up with eyes clear of blood and minds free of nightmares. And the people in the hall?" he added, waving a hand toward the door to the apartment. "Another day or two and they will be released from their restraints, their blood clean and eyes clear."

Celeste's heart thudded so hard in her chest she was afraid the others could hear it. "That makes no sense," she said, her voice almost croaking as she recalled what Glider had said. "Either the Protectorate lied to us about it, or Clarion lied to you about what you're doing. It would hardly be the first human trials conducted under false pretenses."

He shrugged, the dismissal of her statement clear. "Your leaders might bathe in lies on a daily basis, but the body cannot. The monoclonal antibodies which I inject into confirmed Dreamers result in blood samples free of the virus a week to ten days later." He gave her an almost pitying look. "A tongue might distort the truth. But the saliva lubricating it cannot. The people in the apartment above are cured. And those on the other side of the door will be soon, unless you take us from our work." He looked directly into Benji's eyes as he said this. "Or your handlers watching back at home instruct you to kill us."

Aveen started at this. A high-level scientist for the Protectorate would know of their technology, and it was obvious Jiang was world-wise and equally weary, supposing he wasn't lying about being a dead scientist, that for some reason Tofe knew about. Syncing was invisible to those not wearing the lenses Aveen and the others were, but it didn't take a genius with Jiang's background to guess he was being recorded. All syncs were downloaded following completion of the operation, as a means of latent intelligence gathering, and teams were encouraged to perform them for this purpose.

But what will Captain Nest and the others make of what he said? Aveen asked himself. *If even half of what he said is true, we've got serious problems.*

But they did not get the chance to question the man further. The old woman who had been thrown backward over the metal examination table suddenly rose up with the gun in her hands, and with a shriek, began firing.

Two of the bullets slammed into Tofe's chest, knocking him back a step. These did not penetrate but fell to the floor, their momentum halted by his LT suit. Two other shots went wide, one passing over his shoulder to bury itself in the wall, while the fourth slipped under his left arm and pinged off the metal table facing Celeste.

Benji's sync switched off and by reflex Tofe fired at her, and this time a half a dozen Bulldogs struck her center mass and lifted her off her feet. She flew backward and slammed into the wall beside the front door, sliding down it to lay crumpled in a white-coated heap.

"Angie!" screamed the man in front of Celeste, and as he made to run past her to the old woman Celeste pivoted and swung the butt of her rifle up and across his chin. The impact snapped his head to the side, and he teetered in place for a moment before falling and lying still. Hammering on the door and voices outside in the hallway come through in muffled calls, and Tofe backed up with his gun pointed at the door. He reached up to touch his throat.

"Hostile got off several shots but is down now. Celeste took the second man out. But we've got company in the hall trying to get in."

"Shit," Aveen whispered, as the patrol neared the building once more. He flicked off his rifle's safety and lined up the mil dots of his sight on the second man in marching formation. "Secure that woman's weapon and get Dr. Guozhi—Jiang, whoever he is— out of there!"

"Roger that," Tofe said, striding forward to the woman who had fired at him as the banging outside intensified. The gun had flown from her hand as she was hurled back and lay ten feet away. He rolled her onto her back with his foot while covering her with his Scorpion, but it was obvious she was no longer a threat. Her arms flopped out to the sides, and she stared up at the ceiling with the disinterest of the dead. The sight twisted his heart and made his throat cramp up, but he called out: "Hostile is neutralized. Celeste?"

"He's out, but alive," she replied, swinging her rifle onto her back by its strap and flipping the man onto his face. She cinched plastic restraints onto his wrists and stood up from him, pulling her weapon back around. "Benji?"

He didn't answer and both Tofe and Celeste looked to him. He was down on one knee, and his weapon was slung across his back, and at first, Celeste thought he was hit. They rushed to him but pulled up short at seeing what he was doing.

"Damn it," Tofe said, then returned to pointing his Scorpion at the door. It shuddered as something heavy rammed it from outside. He switched his ammunition setting to "eels" and pressed his throat. "Cap'n, target's down. Benji's tending to him. And we've got less than a minute before they're through that door."

"Goddamn it," Aveen hissed, trying to keep his voice down as the patrol passed nearer to the front door across the street. "Do what you can for him. Celeste, grab the intel. If we get back with nothing but a dead body to show for the run, the General will add ours to the tally."

As she hustled over to the computers and plugged in a "Santa Sack" data siphon, Benji pressed gauze to the neck of the dying doctor. The old man was thrashing feebly on the floor with blood pooling around him in a dark red slick, and Benji gritted his teeth.

Fuck. It's a neck wound. He's gone, and there's nothing I can do.

He reached into his left thigh pouch and pulled out a medkit, flipping it open and yanking out a coagulant packet. He tore it open and slung the soaked bandage away from the man's throat, then dashed the dark gray powder onto the slash where the ricocheting bullet had cut a furrow. The dribbling blood slowed to a trickle and then an oozing, and Benji applied a fresh bandage as the front door crashed inward.

Half a dozen people poured in through the hole, and Tofe fired off three eels at their knee height. The flying pods exploded upon contact, and the group lit up as electricity wreathed them in a trio of sparking nets. The wrapping of light winked out a moment later, but it had done its job; the intruders collapsed to the floor in a twitching heap of shocked limbs and arching backs. Other heads poked in through the doorway but quickly withdrew, and Tofe called over his shoulder without taking his eyes from the door: "Breach is sealed for the moment. You got the data yet?"

"Nearly there," Celeste yelled back, as she pulled the cigarette-sized siphon from the third drive and jammed it into a fourth. The "Santa Sack" was so named because it could hold an incredible amount of data in a small size. The downside was it could not do so with discretion. When you plugged in a Sack, you threw everything into it.

"All right, the patrol's passing by," Aveen said into his throat as the six-man team marched in front of the building's entrance. "You guys got lucky they didn't hear those shots and come up to share some of their own."

"There's hostiles in the hallway," Tofe cut in. "If they don't have guns, that will be lucky. Can you take the patrol if you have to?"

"Not without killing them. Eels won't work at this range. Can Dr. Whoever be stabilized?"

Benji sighed in frustration. "Not that I can tell. He took a shot to the neck, and has lost at least two pints already. I'm doing what I can."

"Then quit talking to me," Aveen said, his scope on the right temple of the second man in formation. "I'll give them another minute and either start shooting or running. Rendezvous on the roof in five whatever happens, and bring anything you can."

"Roger that," Benji replied. He pressed the gauze to the doctor's neck with his left hand and gripped the old man's right wrist with his other as Jiang's head lolled back and forth in a daze. Benji released the grip and looked at his right wrist display.

Blood pressure's 82 over 53. The guy's turning hypovolemic.

More shots and screams came from his left, and he spun to see a fresh wave of men and women came hurtling through the doorway, their faces distorted with fury and terror. He was reaching for his rifle when someone grabbed his wrist.

"Wait..."

He looked down and saw the old man clutching at him. "Give... give me... a syringe."

Benji blinked and made a face. He was about to ask what for, but then reached into the medkit and brought one out and handed it to the dying man.

Without a word, the doctor jammed it into the side of his neck, and with great effort, reached across his body to pull back on the plunger. The vial filled with blood, and he pulled the syringe free.

"Take it. Get it... to Nelson. Tell him... it wasn't his... fault."

Benji accepted the small plastic tube as the sound of more crackling shocks filled the room. The eels Tofe fired into the howling crowd lit up the room and made Benji flinch. The man on the floor was past caring, but he had enough strength to point to a corner of the room.

"The plant ... take ... take ..."

He sighed and lay still. Benji took his wrist, but his own displayed a flashing red light and a flatline. He stood up from the dead man and looked to the vial, considering it for a moment. His choice made, he twisted off the needle and pocketed it.

"The target's dead," he said as he pressed his throat. "But he gave me something. Said to take it to Dr. Nelson."

Aveen was breaking down his sniper's rifle when he heard this, as the patrol had turned the corner at the far end of the road. "Take what?"

"His blood."

All three heads turned at that. Tofe's from the doorway where a growing pile of groaning bodies writhed, Celeste's from the computer she was pulling data from, and Aveen's down on the street as he slung his rifle onto his back and prepared to pull on his climbing gloves and knee pads.

"He gave you blood?" Aveen asked, looking up at the fifth floor in confusion.

"Yeah, and a plant," Benji said, jogging over to the glass case where he withdrew the foot-high shrub with yellow flowers that glowed with a faint, creamy light.

Aveen jerked on his climbing gear and ran across the road, as Tofe stared at the plant Benji pulled from the case. He didn't recognize it, but the thought of the parade of plants and creatures that Dr. Nelson tended to in Castle Corvin made it more than a coincidence.

He yelled across the gap to Benji: "He said to give the plant to Nelson? He said that?"

"He didn't get the chance to—watch out!"

Tofe turned to find a massive beast of a man bearing down on him. He brought his gun around—but not fast enough—the ogre grabbed him and hurled him across the room to slam into a pair of the computers Celeste was pulling files from. She yelped and spun around as the big man charged, his direction changing toward her, but just before he reached her, the top right section of the attacker's head exploded. His momentum carried him another few steps before he toppled onto what remained of his face, crushing one of the computer towers beneath him. Celeste twisted to find Benji pointing his Scorpion in one hand and holding the plant in the other.

"I'd say it's time to leave," Benji said, turning to cover the door cleared of faces.

"Yeah," Tofe said, wincing as he rolled to one knee and stood. His suit saved him from a broken back, but it still hurt like hell.

"You all right?" Celeste asked, as he swung his rifle over his shoulder and reached out for one of the three ropes still dangling through the hole in the ceiling.

"My bikini days will suffer a bit because of the bruises," he cracked, his smile showing obvious pain as he pressed the end of the rope to the small of his back to adhere a strong magnetic seal, "but yeah, I'm good. You get all the data?"

She nodded and attached her own rope to her lower spine as Benji stepped forward and did the same with his. He motioned at the lying form of the man Celeste had restrained. "You want to take him?"

She started to consider it, but then a clanking noise by the door reached her ears. She looked and swore. "Shit! Artillery!"

The massive cannon the pair of men clunked down in the hallway with the barrel poking through the breach was meant to fire on tanks. But the masks the men wore told her that it wasn't carrying the usual ordinance.

"*Smoker!*" Tofe shouted, and without waiting for a response he gave his rope two quick tugs and was pulled upward through the hole in the ceiling. Benji and Celeste followed almost as quickly just as the *BOOM* of the cannon sounded. This was accompanied by a loud *whoosh*, and the trio threw themselves sideways from the hole as an enormous mushroom of green gas erupted from below.

They released the cables on their lower backs and sprinted away from the hole, as the cloud of sickly vapor settled over the rim of it. The heavier-than-air nature meant it couldn't follow them, and they watched as it coalesced and slowly slid back out of sight like some grotesque pudding.

Tofe looked at the two beside him and asked if they were all right.

"Yeah, but not for long," Celeste said, tucking the data siphon into an interior pocket of her tactical vest. "They know where we are and we'd better get to the roof while we can. This apartment is hardly defensible."

Not to mention, I don't want the family we tranqed caught in the cross-fire like the man who didn't want to be rescued, she thought.

A minute later found them running through the door leading out onto the roof, just as Aveen threw himself over the parapet. Fat drops of rain pattered down in irregular patterns, and the sky above them lashed with lightning that outlined the bulging clouds. Aveen jogged toward them as he pulled off his climbing gloves and immediately recognized something was wrong.

"Company?"

Tofe nodded back at the door. "Yeah. Any minute."

"Then barricade it while I call in the transport."

Benji and Tofe nodded and turned back toward the opening, but Aveen called out to Celeste. She jogged over as they pulled their guns around and shot out the metal bracings of an air conditioning unit, then began muscling it to the door. It screeched as they dragged it over the concrete roof, and Aveen used the noise to cover his words.

"You and I are going to talk later. When we're in quarantine. Understand?"

She opened her mouth to reply, but he held up a hand. "Not here. Later."

She nodded and remained silent. He leaned closer as though checking her for wounds. "Can you scrub the sync? The one where he says he's got the cure and is a dead man? You were always better than me at ICE."

She blinked. The weight of what he was asking of her landed hard, and as he pulled back to stare, she let out a breath.

But she nodded. "It won't be perfect. If anyone looks at it too closely—"

"Good," he said, his voice louder as it returned to normal and cutting off her caution. "Get over there and help cover our exit while I confirm the pickup."

She turned and jogged over, her mind racing. She put her shoulder into pushing the heavy thermostat unit the last few feet to the stairwell door. They made it just in time. As the 130-kilo cube of metal, fans, and wiring wedged against the door, heavy feet pounded up the stairs and crashed into the barrier. The door opened an inch, and the unit shrieked as it went backward, and the three agents shoved it forward once more.

"One minute to pickup!" Aveen shouted, and Benji told the others to go to stand with their leader.

"I'll keep them from pushing the door open until transport gets here."

"What if they shoot through it and hit you?" Celeste asked.

"Then shoot back!" he yelled, as heavy blows sent the door shuddering in its frame. Benji sat with his back against the air conditioning unit, and sure enough, a break in the ramming against the door was filled by a hail of bullets shredding the metal. They all flew over his head and the other three dodged far to the left side of the roof so they were not in the line of fire.

"How long?" Tofe asked, his rifle aimed at the door. Celeste followed suit, each squinting to bring the door closer and increase their chances of shooting over and around their teammate should the barrier break down.

"30 seconds!"

Half a minute later, a low humming came from the west, and all heads looked up to see a shadow moving through the night sky. It was painted by the flashes of lightning from the storm settling over Bucharest, and the ten-person special operations combat transport came down to hover 15 meters over their heads.

"Benji! Move your ass!" Aveen shouted.

The younger Agent did, rolling up onto one knee and then to his feet, sprinting forward as the belly of the transport opened and ropes fell out. They each grabbed one and jammed it onto their backs, holding it in place to increase the magnetic seal. Just as Aveen looked skyward and gave the pilot the thumbs up, an explosion rocked the roof. The door blasted outward and took a large chunk of the thermostat unit with it, and Celeste and Benji spun to fire a burst of Bulldogs and eels into the crowd of heav-

ily-armed men who poured through the smoking hole and
around the wreckage of the temporary doorstop. Tofe added a
few live rounds at the feet of the men to drive them back, as the
rubber balls and sticky electric charges slammed into and fried
them.

A moment later, the transport lifted up on a surge of its magnetic
motor and the four agents in black swung away into the darkness
toward the western mountains. A few seconds after this saw
them pulled up into the belly of the ship and the door closed,
leaving only an oblong shadow for the men still standing on the
rooftop to fire at. Then only empty sky and cloud-to-cloud
lighting could be seen, and they ceased firing as rain began
lashing the sleeping city.

14

RESPONSIBILITY BY THE NUMBERS

*G*eneral Aepal stood in his office and considered his bookshelf as the computer secured the room. The lights dimmed and the glowing chairs showing the other world leaders appeared as the clouds of nanites drifted up from the floor to coalesce into the full panel of the World Security Council.

They began bickering almost at once, detailing the pushback each was getting from not only those outside their respective Fences, but even within. "Recruitment for the military and police is way down," the Northern Europe minister said, his tone angry. "And the Enhanced Security Forces for the academies are seeing fewer and fewer agents emerging."

"Cicadas are washing out right and left," another one griped. "My school's current class is 22% lower than it was the previous year!"

"Not to mention there are increasing assaults all over the globe by Clarion's cells," a third cut in.

"They seem to know just how to hit us," the Canadian minister said, her gaze menacing and suspicious as she looked around the panel. "That can only mean someone inside is collaborating with them. Someone in your schools or forces is feeding them intelligence."

"Perhaps," Aepal conceded, still considering the books. "But it could just as easily be coming from your own people."

As she began to snarl this was preposterous, another man proposed a thorough purging of disloyal personnel, and an intense round of PSYOP sessions with the *mencist* corps. General Aepal sighed and shook his head. "I don't mean to give offense, but that isn't the way to deal with people. Especially ones you ask to sacrifice their lives for a nation, should it be required. I was a soldier in the early days of the plague; I saw what we had to do to overcome the enemy. And it wasn't accomplished by cutting our own throats."

"No, it was accomplished by locking ourselves in bubbles and letting the rest of the world burn in fever dreams," the Ukrainian leader said, his tone flat. "Dreams we dispersed."

"Which is the only reason the world isn't a charred wasteland," Aepal sighed, pinching the bridge of his nose. "And the only reason it's still holding together today."

"Which is why we've got to stop that cure!" the Canadian leader said, slapping her desk with a sound that reverberated around Aepal's office. "They'll see it as salvation. They'll think it will make everything go back to the way it was before."

"Before *us*, you mean," the Mediterranean minister added, his expression neutral.

"Of course that's what I mean!" she snapped, turning to look at him. "I'm not going to apologize for saving this world from collapsing under the weight of 10 billion people! I grew up starving in a one-bedroom shithole in Toronto, and now that place is a goddamned paradise! 26 million winnowed down to a million and a half, and look at it! Unemployment's at 2%. No one's in line outside of a soup kitchen. Hell, 'Public Assistance' consists of free education and a hefty UBI. You think that'll last if those ingrates overrun the Fences with full immunity from this damned cure?"

"Do we even know the population outside the barriers?" the minister of the Amazon Biological Protectorate asked. "The nearest my people can guess for our region is 50 million. Which if true, is 90% less than it was antebellum."

"So what you're saying is to let them all in, is that it?" the Canadian minister shot back.

He offered a slight, unruffled shrug in his gray tailored suit. "Three decades have reduced the species in every corner of the globe. We began this operation all those years ago when we altered the virus Dr. Nelson and Jiang created, with the goal of lowering the population to 3 billion. If we've done it, what is the argument for maintaining the DOX?"

Silence settled over the room as the question went unanswered. As it continued Aepal withdrew an old leather-bound book from the middle shelf. He held it in both hands and considered its faded red cover as the other leaders watched.

"You know, I never wanted to lead. I was born into a family who saw enlistment as a duty. Being an officer was never what my father or grandfather aspired to. To serve, yes. To command the details of that service? No."

He opened the book and turned to a page near the end.

> *I am at the pinnacle, free to do as I please. I would be*
> *excused by my peers for it, by my past exploits and*
> *adventures, and perhaps even by those yet unborn*

who look back on the edicts and choices which
resulted from them. By this measure I am just. For
justice is that which the authority of the land deems it
to be. I am that authority, but I am not the ideal such
an office suggests. I am a man. And men are both
fallible and of limited years. When the end of their
time nears, they clutch at it as a raft in a turbulent
sea. And yet, that time comes all the same. I cannot
look to the future for praise, nor to the past for
reconciliation. This moment alone is that which I
truly command. And I know my service is in the past,
and the closing of my eyes in the future. I therefore
choose to lay down my sword and rod in the present. I
choose to let the past be what others decree and the
years to come what others develop. I will remain
a man.

He closed the book and laid it on his desk. His eyes rested on it for several seconds, and then he turned to the panel of holographic world leaders.

"This is a biography of a man who lived long ago. His name was Cincinnatus, and he began life as a patrician in the nobility of ancient Rome. His son was violently opposed to the growing strength of the common people, and he actively sought to destroy their attempts at increased power and legal protection. He ended up killing at least one of the peasants in a public forum where they were advocating for what amounted to what we might call a declaration of independence. He fled into exile and was condemned to death in absentia. The legal proceedings of this effectively bankrupted his father, and Cincinnatus went off into his own quiet retirement to manage a tiny farm.

"But when war and disaster threatened the Republic, the rulers chose to grant him unlimited power. He accepted this in a famous scene in which one hand gripped the handle of his plow and the other the issue delivered by a group of senators which literally placed him above the law. He would hold it for 15 days, and then when called upon again, for three weeks."

"That is all fascinating," the Canadian woman said, her voice flat and expression not even attempting respect, "but we are talking about the present. You know, the part your idol said was the only one he could control?"

Aepal sighed and went on, not sparing her a look. "He could have held onto his power and done as he wished. The empire owed him that. And the loyalty he earned by saving the troops in several campaigns would have seen him as Caesar, nearly five centuries before Julius would cross the Rubicon. But he gave it up, and we venerate him for it. He only took the job because his nation needed him. We only took ours because the world needed us to."

He looked to the Amazonian leader. "It is a fair question to ask why we should not do as Cincinnatus did. He called it when he said future generations would praise him for it. And as you noted: there is every reason to believe the antebellum population that crushed governments and cultures beneath its gravity has been lessened to an extraordinary degree. It is the logical time to lay down our own rod and sword."

The leaders adjusted their positions in the gap that followed. Several leaned forward slightly in anticipation, while others tilted away with dubious expressions. "I was pushed into a leadership position that no one in my family had any experience with," Aepal said, striding slowly before them, his eyes on the floor or ceiling but not them. "Like Cincinnatus, I was called to protect my nation in a time of unprecedented upheaval. And I can look back on him as he predicted I would, judging him through the lens of history."

"And what do you see?" the woman ministering Southeast Asia asked, her voice smooth and tone soft.

He turned to face them. "I see a world he could never have imagined. And its risk has run far longer than the few weeks he had to endure. Three decades on, our war is only now becoming won. But laying down our arms and authority will not be seen by future generations as noble. The passing of the torch will only be viewed as casting it down to start a new fire."

Now all leaned forward. "So what is it you propose?" the Canadian minister asked, her voice free of scorn. Now her eyes shone with eagerness.

"That we do what he was too weak to do: use our authority to build a newer, better world. We have already begun, but the wolves at the gate are pressing forward to overwhelm the protectorates. They've infiltrated many places and positions, and it is only a matter of time before they complete the destruction Cincinnatus's descendants experienced with the fall of the empire to the Goths. And make no mistake, ladies and gentlemen," he added, "the dark age that would follow our fall would be far more lasting. Perhaps even permanent."

"The solution?" the Polynesian minister asked.

Aepal nodded, as though deciding the ultimate end of their debate. "That we allow the cure to go ahead."

This caused an uproar. Everyone began speaking at once, and Aepal did not try to yell them down. It was not his way. After half a minute of laughter, shouts, cries of 'madness!' and other upheaval, he raised his hands in a calming gesture.

"If you will permit me, I will present my reasoning for this approach."

The cool, unperturbed tone had its intended effect. The other leaders growled and grumbled, but all soon grew silent. Aepal nodded and turned back to the bookshelf. He withdrew another book but did not open it.

"The intelligence that my team brought back after the failed mission to capture Dr. Jiang is why I propose this. Our analysis of the files has allowed my people to work out the nature of the cure Clarion is manufacturing. It is this very tool they believe will unite the world against us which will prove their undoing."

"I suggest you get to your point, general," the North African minister said, his eyes hard. "And I hope you will do so without resorting to another reading of some long-dead sage."

Aepal smiled, his mouth widening beneath his beard but not revealing his teeth.

"If Clarion was to disperse a cure out into the world, people would doubtless turn against us. It might take weeks or months, but it would happen."

"But why not take out the stores of it?" the Polynesian minister asked. "We know where most of their bases are, they lack the power sources adequate to maintain their own Fences."

Aepal shook his head. "No. It's clear from Dr. Jiang's files that the stores are decentralized and equally spread across the globe. Just as Clarion itself is scattered and nontraditional, so too is their supply chain. Take out one, and a dozen more still exist with no direct link to the one you illuminated. And frankly, we don't have the numbers to hit them all at once. If only one escaped, they would produce more doses. And the public catching wind of our action would be a faster doom than anything Clarion could do to us directly."

"So what do you suggest, General?" the Amazonian leader asked, his tone respectful.

He raised his second book. This one bore a simple faded brown cover and was very old.

"This is *The Art of War*, by Sun Tzu. It was written 2,000 years ago, and its lessons are no less relevant than what we face today." He looked at the panel and recited from memory.

> *When facing a larger force, and one determined to outlast you, you cannot charge in head first. You must weaken them from within so that they fall upon each other, allowing you to move in at your leisure. The best way to do this is to set a discord amongst their ranks, and if they are too tightly connected an enemy and so not subject to such ploys, then you must utilize the citizens they rely upon for their food and shelter. Turn the native population against them, and they will fall. When done properly, you will not need to engage them in battle at all.*

He set the book down on his desk. "We are facing an enemy that is no less ruthless than ourselves, and far more experienced in the world beyond our fences. We cannot hope to overcome them in direct confrontation, regardless of our technical superiority. We must break them from within, but as my counterpart from two millennia ago noted: They are too determined a force for such ploys. We therefore must utilize those whom they depend on. We must let them administer the cure to all of the DOX."

"But that's insane!" snapped the Canadian woman. "Once they disperse the cure, the population will love them. They will turn against *us*, not Clarion!"

Aepal nodded. "Again, in time, that would be the case. But that same population, were they to receive the cure and discover it was not their salvation but an even greater curse, they would turn upon those who gave it to them. But by then, it would be too late."

The Southeast Asian minister considered him, his expression calculating. "You already have begun preparations for this, haven't you?"

Aepal nodded. "Once we determined the genetic sequences of their cure, it was a simple matter of inserting a corrosive sequence within it. In this case, we simply attached several chains of amino acids which work to corrupt the vector itself. The result is the most intense presentations of *dreamscape*, and these occur at a 100% rate."

Everyone on the panel was quiet for a moment, letting this sink in. They were shocked and staggered by this concept, as well as the ramifications.

The Asian minister recovered first. "What you are suggesting, General," he said, his voice soft and his eyes watching the man beside his desk without blinking, "is to reinfect the general population. But with the consequences far beyond the original. You are saying we should poison all the people beyond the Fences."

Aepal glared at the man, his control finally cracking. "Yes, that is precisely what I am proposing." He opened his arms at all of them, his voice hard. "How did we come here, people? How did we arrive at this state? Overpopulation, pure and simple. That's why there was a war in the first place. That's why *dreamscape* had to be released as a way to combat it and to force people to follow our laws and our rules. So what happens if the cure is released and then people overthrow us? They will go right back to what they were before. It might take a few decades, maybe a century or two. But they would once again creep up to 10 billion people. Once again, war would come to them, and once again some group of people like ourselves would be forced to do the unthinkable in order to combat it."

"What I am proposing," he went on, his expression softening and growing more thoughtful, "is to be practical. If we know 150 years from now that 5 billion people will die because we decided to give up our power as Cincinnatus did, then we are responsible for those deaths. If we kill off all of those outside of the fences— and from the best estimates this amounts to no more than half a billion people—we would save ten times that many. Our grand-children and great grandchildren would live in a world that was in balance. They would live in the world that we have created today," he added, his eyes turning to the Canadian minister, "without having to go through the back and forth, the up and down, the nightmare of alternating plague and plenty. Consider this plan carefully, and then tell me I'm a monster. Work out for yourselves what I'm saying, and then tell me what we must do."

The room was silent for a full minute, before the Australian minister spoke up. Her voice was quiet and composed, and her eyes were clear if somewhat reddened.

"As much as I would like to say this is a flawed and monstrous proposition, the past is the surest guide of what our future would be should we not adopt it. Whether it be Cincinnatus or Sun Tzu, those people knew when to quit and when to fight. We must learn from them and apply those lessons in our own version of the present which will one day become a future."

She closed her eyes with a pained expression and let out a sigh. "I call for a vote on the proposal to insert a corrupting sequence into the cure. And allow it to be dispersed into the outside population."

She looked around at the faces, as they cycled through various expressions of concern, contempt, and wariness. "I vote yes," the Canadian minister said, responding first.

"As do I," said the sub-Saharan minister.

All in favor?" asked the Southeast Asian leader.

One by one, hands were raised, until only the Amazonian minister remained. Aepal looked to him.

"Julio? What do you wish to say?"

At first the man did not respond, then he sighed. "I cannot fault the math of this proposition, and yet the morality of it is very obviously flawed. We might preserve an appropriate number of people, and those individuals would have a comfortable balance of resources and living space. But how do we reconcile the loss? To maintain anything within ourselves approaching humanity? How do we allow for the dispersal of something we know is going to kill 90% of what remains of our species?"

Aepal looked from one face to another and saw discomfort. No one spoke. So he did.

"We are the only species on this planet with the ability to affect others on such a scale. For far too long we have caused the extinction of millions of birds, reptiles, and pretty much every other type. The proposal I make affects only ourselves. The cure would be transmissible only among us, unlike *dreamscape* which jumped between species. So when I say that the world to come would be a healed one, it is as much because no other species has to suffer for our mistakes, as it will be for the better one we build with a manageable population. Only humans would die. This allows every other one to recover, along with those who remain inside of our fences."

Julio's hand still did not rise, and Aepal frowned. "Your protectorate used to be the 'lungs of the planet.' The rainforests covered
thousands of square miles, and did so for millions of years. Until
we came along and slashed and burned to make way for fast food
and dairy cows. In less than a century you lost three-quarters of
that breath. And it wasn't because of anything the jungle did. No
apes or lizards or plants did it. We did. If you were the represen-
tative of the trees, your hand would be the first to lift. If you were
any other species—any goddamned bug or bird or whatever that
humans devastated in those woods—you would have been the
one to call for this vote."

The hands were in the air still, and the South American minister
considered his own, palm up, toward him. He brought them
together and rubbed as though washing something from them.
Then with a sigh, he raised his right hand.

Aepal stared around, his breath coming out in a slow exhalation
of finality, of commitment. "Yes, it is as it should be. And I assure
you that our sacrifice will be seen in time as the right one, just as
you all have seen it to be now."

He turned away as the hands fell. "And how will we implement
this corruption?" the Slavic minister asked, his hand slowly
rubbing his bearded chin, the look of a man suddenly much older
on his face.

"Sacrifice is what I said we must do, and it is one which will hurt.
Hurt deeply," he added, his expression tired and sad.

"I am sending the details of what you must do, along with the
technical aspects of the cure's addition. You must produce it
quickly in under two days and be ready to disperse it in less than
72 hours. The targets will be the Clarion outposts in your respective districts, which you all have the locations of."

He made for the door and one of the leaders called out to ask where he was going.

He stopped with his hand on the panel that would slide up the section of wall into an opening and half looked back.

"I go to make the sacrifice in person. I hope each of you will have the strength to do likewise. We owe them that much."

15

QUARANTINE QUESTIONS

The following morning Celeste opened her eyes and found them on a white, featureless ceiling. She blinked and rolled over.

Right. Still here for another day.

She looked to the bed beside hers and found Aveen lying awake and staring up at the ceiling. "Hey. You didn't sleep?"

He spoke without looking at her. "Yeah, a little."

She looked around and saw Tofe and Benji in their respective single beds beneath their own airtight plastic tents. Dr. Nelson sat at a computer terminal on the far end of the room with his back to them, his head whipping back and forth between the screen and the metal table beside him where numerous papers, plastic trays, and other experiment materials lay. Among them was the small shrub with gauzy, faintly-glimmering yellow flowers the team had taken from Dr. Jiang's lab. Celeste watched the old scientist's back and smiled.

At least someone's happy. The guy hasn't stopped running around since we dropped off the plant and the Sack's data.

"I just can't believe he didn't contact me. All these years he's been alive, and nothing. Not a word."

"Who? Dr. Jiang?"

He frowned as though she had asked a stupid question. "No, Glider."

Celeste twisted in her bed to face him. He looked up at the ceiling with his fingers laced behind his head and sighed. "He must have his reasons," she said. "And considering he's working with Clarion, they must be good ones."

"Or else he's a traitor," Aveen said, his jaw tightening. "It wouldn't be the first time an agent went over to the wrong side."

Celeste nodded. It was something she had considered from the beginning, when the nanite form of the vanished operative appeared on the Bucharest rooftop.

"But Dr. Jiang went over to them as well. And it's pretty hard to see everything he said in that apartment as just a lie to get us to take his plant back to Dr. Nelson. And I'm sorry," she added, sitting up and crossing her arms and legs as she faced him, "but when you're dying, you don't usually use your last moments to pass on some dick move trick you won't be around to see. Hardcore cultists might die for whatever they believe in, and I'd like to think we all would to save people. But Jiang was a bitter, cynical scientist. They're not known for their altruism."

"The thing that sells it for me is the blood."

Both Aveen and Celeste turned in their beds to find Benji lying on one side with his head supported on his left hand.

"His blood?" Aveen asked.

"Yeah. He could have just said the files Celeste was downloading had the genetic sequence of the cure. Why use his last strength to jab himself in the neck to hand over a sample of it?"

"Because he couldn't be sure what would happen to the files once we got back here," Tofe said, his voice quiet and thoughtful in the last bed in the line. This caused the other three to look at him, and he went on. "He didn't trust Aepal to do the right thing, and he couldn't be sure of us. But the old lab partner who he created *dreamscape* with and felt terrible guilt about doing so? Yeah, he could trust Nelson."

Benji frowned. "Yeah, okay. I get that. But why give us the blood? Doc Nelson says the plant has unique genetic anomalies which somehow allow it to cross with human, human…" he rolled his eyes and looked disgusted with himself, "what was that he said he used on the people? Something bodies?"

"Monoclonal antibodies," Tofe said. "The moAb Dr. Jiang mentioned. And that's part of why he gave his blood. It's unique for each person, so it wasn't enough to just hand over the formula in the Sack. It had to be proven to work in the individual. Jiang was successfully inoculated with the cure Clarion came up with, and his blood proved it."

Benji made a face at him. "Since when do you know all this science stuff?"

Tofe threw his legs over the side of the bed and sat up. "When I was stuck in here for a couple of days with Dr. Nelson after the final exam, we talked about his work and how he had been unable to develop a cure even after three decades. He told me he made it with Dr. Jiang, who was supposed to be dead from cancer."

"But why would they lie to us about getting him from that apartment?" Benji asked. "Why not just say it was Dr. Jiang?"

"You mean the same guys who told Dr. Nelson he was dead?" Celeste asked, her tone withering. "And who very likely know that Jiang made a cure to *dreamscape* and not a new form of it? Yeah, I can't think of any reason why they'd keep that to themselves."

Aveen sat up and let out a long breath. The others turned to face him and it was clear he had come to a decision by the resolute expression he wore. "All right. We've got one more day in here before quarantine expires and we're set to join the rest of the agents in a massive raid on the DOX to find the weapon Clarion's about to drop on our heads. Except there is no weapon. They're trying to hand over the cure to *dreamscape*. And it looks like the Protectorate wants to stop that."

"Dr. Jiang said as much when he spat back the offer to rescue him," Celeste said. "He said they would put him in prison or kill him, rather than welcome him back."

"Which means they must know about the cure," Aveen said, lowering his voice and his expression darkening. "And they must have known it existed before we went out there to extract him. They wanted him to give it to them, most likely to develop and distribute themselves to take credit."

"But won't they be able to do that now anyway, since they've got the files?" Benji asked.

Aveen shrugged. "You would think so. But maybe there's a missing piece to the formula. That would be another reason for the blood and plant to go straight to Nelson."

"And maybe it's just the Protectorate deciding to bury the evidence along with Clarion," Tofe said, shaking his head. "Even if they had the cure, they couldn't get away with not sending it out to all people in the DOX. And once they were all free of *dreamscape*, other stories in which the Protectorate was shown to be dirty would have to come out. Think of that old scientist who lost her husband and family. The one who shot at us in Jiang's apartment."

"Angie," Celeste said quietly.

"Right, her," Tofe said. "We've all heard stories of the Protectorate hurting innocent people over the years. Usually the newslinks are scrubbed of any of it, but people whisper stuff that's hard to ignore. And Angie was screaming and shooting at us—you can't gloss over that shit. Who knows how many stories like that are out there? And if the cure was handed out to everyone, the Fences would have to go down. No way the Protectorate could round up everyone who had a bad story to tell once there was no reason to have a barrier separating people."

Aveen twisted to look at Nelson. His back was to them and he continued to yank papers to him and type quickly on his keyboard as he looked at the screen.

"All right. This is what's going to happen. We can agree that the mission to the DOX is about something they're not telling us. And it's useless to bring it up with anyone above us, as it would likely just earn us all plasma holes in our heads and a P.R.-friendly obituary."

"So what do you want to do?" Celeste asked, as she and the others leaned toward him.

"We're going into the DOX, like we're expected to do. And once we're there, Glider will find some way of contacting us. We've got to figure out a way to get to him and hear the rest of the story."

"Or he already told you how to find him," Tofe said, his gaze thoughtful. "Didn't his message on the roof say something about Aveen always bugging him for the answer to a question?"

She nodded. "Yeah, but I didn't hear most of that part." She looked to Aveen. "Do you know what he was talking about?"

Aveen stared off into the distance, far beyond the borders of the infirmary's walls. "This place isn't what it seems. It was always meant for war and to display power, but not in how we use it." He craned his neck to the ceiling, following the line of the smooth white sides to where it flattened out.

"Behind this plastic and concrete are stones a thousand years old. It's hidden beneath the modern, sanitized surface. But it's there."

Benji shot a sideways look to Celeste and Tofe. "Yeah, okay. Sure there's the original stonework on the other side of the walls here. But so what?"

Aveen brought his gaze down and looked at him. "I was never good with history. It was Glider's passion. He took to it after General Aepal gave a speech at his being named the youngest agent in the Protectorate's history. Just 17," he murmured, his eyes looking back at the man who was his idol. Dead and mourned, and now resurrected like Jiang.

Aveen snapped out of it and looked back to Benji, his expression intense. "This castle was built by a man who was living in a time of war. In a time where there were no flight suits or magnetic shields. It was all hand-to-hand combat. Steel and swords, blood and backstabbing."

Benji raised an eyebrow. "Yeah, the 14th century wasn't what one could call a 'happy-feely' time. What's your point?"

"The point is," Aveen snapped, leaning toward him within his plastic cube, "that when I was a kid, the idea of learning secret history fascinated me. I came from the countryside, and we had no library and few books. It burned in the first years of the Plague War. The only things I had to read were put out by the Protectorate. Tales of great victories against Clarion, although it wasn't called that then. They didn't have a name when I was a kid slaving in the fields west of Arad on the Hungarian border. So when I came here, to this place," he waved a hand around, "the feeling of being surrounded by centuries of something lasting really hit me. And Glider knew a lot of the castle's past."

Celeste cocked her head at him. "But there was something he wouldn't tell you?"

Aveen nodded. "Yeah. The castle supposedly had a hidden tunnel the builders put in. It was below ground, I was certain. And Glider knew!" he grinned and shook his head. "But he wouldn't tell me where it was. No matter how much I bugged and begged him, he never gave up the entrance. He never said where it came out."

No one spoke for a while. Then Benji broke the silence in a quiet, thoughtful tone.

"This castle was built by John Hunyadi. But he never used it as the true seat of his power. That was in a castle nearer to Bucharest."

The three others turned to him. "So what?" Tofe asked. "If you're saying he built a tunnel to get to his real stronghold in case the castle's defenses were breached, that's insane. Nobody's going to build a tunnel over 500 kilometers long!"

"Stick to science, kid," Benji said, giving him a dismissive grin. "This isn't your area."

He stood from the bed and stretched, his plain white gown shifting as he raised his hands to the limit of his plastic cube. He brought his hands down and began speaking again, this time mostly to himself. "Hunyadi had half a dozen castles built after he was named regent of the area for defending Romania against the Turks. He wasn't here all that often, but a lot of other people were. So they would have cared more about the tunnel. They would have been the ones to keep it operational. Maybe even were the ones who built it."

He began pacing back and forth beside his bed, his voice growing more agitated as he worked out the mystery. Celeste thought he looked like Dr. Nelson, his manic energy emerging as the solution unfolded.

"Castle Corvin's been modified over the centuries, right up until today. Running water replaced the privies, the bricks plasticked over, the fireplaces left as ornaments while central air was put in. The people who made these changes did it for their particular needs and at their particular times. But a tunnel? That had to be constructed when you couldn't just hop on a transport and fly off, or even into a car. When you got to the end of a tunnel you had to disappear in a low-tech way. You had to hop on a horse."

Tofe folded his arms at his friend, one corner of his mouth twisted up in a smile. "All right, so what? It doesn't take a genius to guess the tunnel's old. Probably close to when the castle was built, if it wasn't made by Hunyadi himself."

"Exactly!" Benji crowed, grinning at him. "But it must have been pointing at what the builder considered a safer location than Corvin. If he stepped out of the tunnel's exit and hopped on a horse, that means he could only get 20-50 klicks before the animal died of exhaustion."

"Which means if we can find where the tunnel comes out, we can follow where it points to some other structure within that distance!" Aveen said, his voice loud. He realized his volume and turned to look at Dr. Nelson. The old scientist had turned to look at them, his eyebrows raised.

"I know you folks are eager to get out of here," he said, his expression knowing and his tone firm, "but I'll thank you to keep your voice down. It isn't good for the room's other residents to have sudden loud noises. It upsets them."

Celeste looked to the row of glass cages and saw that several creatures were looking at Aveen with wide, frightened eyes.

"Yes, I'm sorry, doctor," he said, his expression apologetic. The old man turned away, and Aveen looked back to Benji and spoke in a low voice.

"Let's take this back-to-front. Forget about where the tunnel would start inside the castle. God knows I've looked over every inch of the place and found bupkis. What castles are within riding distance, in any direction?"

Tofe nodded. "Yeah, I get it. If we know where the place the builder could've ridden to, we can line it up with Corvin and find the exit."

Celeste thought this clever as they started to discuss what they knew of Castle Corvin's immediate surroundings, but she asked why not just type in the search in the topographical database when they were released the next day. "Because someone might figure out why we were looking," Aveen said. "And once we figure it out, we don't want anyone following us."

"Why not?" Tofe asked. "It'll be a simple matter of breaking away from the other teams in the DOX when we're carrying out the operation."

Rather than Aveen, it was Celeste who answered. "Because we're going to be meeting Glider on his home turf. And if they figure out where he is—and he's probably with a lot of the senior

Clarion leaders—they would probably just drop a quarter-pounder on us all to finish off what Dr. Jiang's death started."

The image of a quarter-megaton guided missile obliterating them all and the answers they were seeking flashed across each of their minds, and all understood why the operation had to be completely covert.

Benji had not said anything since deciding their target was within a radius of under 50 kilometers, but now he grinned. Aveen saw it and asked what was so funny.

"Glider was a genius," he answered, his teeth showing as his mouth stretched further. "And you're an idiot."

"Excuse me?" Aveen said, raising an eyebrow.

"A moron, a nincompoop, a yahoo. You should've known who built the tunnel long before Glider had to use it to escape from Corvin."

Aveen blinked. "He disappeared on a mission to the DOX."

"Yeah, and those two cadets' families were told their kids died fighting for the Protectorate. No, he used the tunnel to escape. And I'm betting he never told you because he didn't want you following him. He was protecting you. Probably why he never contacted you all these years."

"All right," Tofe said, holding up a hand before Aveen could speak. "So who built the tunnel, Mr. History? Where does it point to?"

Benji's expression lost its mirth and he grew more serious. "It was built by the most famous—I should say infamous—Romanian who ever lived. And it points to the castle he built by the literal blood, sweat, and tears of his enemies."

His teammates looked at each other, all wearing uncertain expressions.

"Who?" Celeste asked.

Benji sat down on the bed and let out a breath. "The son of the dragon himself. Vlad Dracul. And the castle we're going to? Poenari, in the haunted forests of the Argeş River valley, close to the Făgăraş Mountains. The real Castle Dracula."

16

ENTROPY

*C*aptain Nest stood in the castle's Great Hall the following morning and looked out over the faces filling the room. The massive space of the thousand-year-old castle was a strange contrast of ancient and modern: super-efficient halogen lamps recessed inside bricks hand-molded centuries before the harnessing of electricity; overhead the high vaulted ceiling was ribbed by oak beams bent by the lost process of water welding. Beneath them stood three long wooden tables that once sat knights and lords in tunics and armor with swords resting beside their plates. Now they hosted soldiers of a different sort: implants that magnified sound and light were surgically a part of the men and women who occupied the benches smoothed by countless sittings, and clothes that halted weapons by dispersing the force of their arrival into invisible bursts of kinetic energy had replaced hammered iron and steel.

Not everyone wore LT suits, however. Some were tasked with infiltration, and these individuals were sheathed in the smooth, tight-fitting black bodysuits that caught the power of incoming death and turned it into invisible force that fanned out on the wind. Other teams wore more conventional body armor, the Kevlar and spider silk-infused titanium of their mesh and plates halting attacks by virtue of its incredible strength rather than catching and redirecting them. The morning light pouring down from the series of stained glass windows high up on the walls of the hall caught on both types of protection, painting soft colors across the long and short-range weapons assigned to the teams.

The dichotomy of old and new was not lost on Captain Nest as she stood on a stage before the three tables running the length of the room. Each held twenty agents; some from the most recent class that saw Aveen and his team added to the ranks, as well as a dozen from previous ones. They talked in low whispers, hunched over their meals and drinks as though worried about eavesdroppers. Others stood beside their seats and laughed loudly as they conversed, not worried in the least.

They all seem so young, she thought, watching their faces and thinking of how many of them she had trained over the years. The truly immature were in another section of the castle, those Cicadas who had not yet accrued the credits to qualify for graduation. They were not going to be part of the upcoming assault and had not yet completed the training that would have seen them through it. Their day was yet to come.

And will they see it? she wondered. *If the operation goes as it should, will there be a need for any of us? Will there be any future agents, or the ones who train them?*

But when General Aepal stepped into the room from a side door at the far end of the hall, she cleared her mind of such thoughts and nodded at a guard standing on one end of the stage. The man turned and called for order.

"Agents! Eyes front!"

All those at the tables, sitting or standing, immediately ceased what they were doing and sat down in their places or turned away from their conversation partner. Once all eyes were on her she raised her hands.

"Thank you. Let's get right into it." She turned to her left, her fingers manipulating the air before her. The section of stone wall of the enormous chamber above the fireplace shimmered and a 30 foot by 25-foot blank white screen materialized, covering the face of the rock.

"Operation Northwoods will be a joint operation carried out across the globe by the Protectorates' Agent corps, as well as a large number of police and military units. While the regular soldiers will go into the DOX with the express purpose of attacking conventional weapons caches and military targets, ours will be more specific."

She typed several keys on her invisible pad, and the screen morphed into a view of Earth. Several dozen glowing red dots appeared scattered across the globe, and rings pulsed outward from them to emphasize their position on the map.

"These are our targets. They are the locations where Clarion is producing their new plague, which we've codenamed *entropy*. While we cannot know for certain its effects on the human body, from the intelligence we've recovered and applied to several dozen biological simulations, it appears that the virus attacks the body's central nervous system. The presentation is likely to be different depending on the person, but the result is the same: slow and certain chaos."

She typed again and the screen showed a virtual man, nude save for a pair of colored briefs. He stared straight ahead at the camera and showed no emotion. A panel on his left showed three measurements, their dials all firmly in the lowest green sections. But as those seated at the table watched, the man's expression changed. His face twitched, and he began to tremble.

"As you can see," Nest said, her eyes on the digital man, "the virus initially causes a loss in muscular control. Spasms and jerks occur within one hour of infection, and these build as the pathogen takes hold."

The man on the screen began to increasingly shake and distort, his arms and legs dodging this way and that until he appeared as though a puppeteer was angry with his performance. The man's mouth opened and shut, his fists clenched and exploded open, and his body began to arch and flail.

"Not a pretty sight," Nest said, her expression dark. "You will note the dramatic increase in acetylcholine as the muscular system descends into a state of hyperactivity. The data also suggests that *entropy* produces an effect similar to an overdose of scopolamine, which causes severe delusions and hallucinations in the affected person."

The man on the screen was wild now, his contorting body cracking his own limbs and joints in his panic and rage. The expression on his face was also terrifying. The frothing mouth, the bloodshot eyes, and the silent scream he was continually emitting gave everyone in the hall a twist in the stomach or a chill along their spine.

"This is what we are heading out in force to stop, people," Nest said, tapping keys to end the demonstration. The man driven to physical and mental madness faded with a last flail and bellow, and the screen returned to show the calmly turning planet.

"Your mission is to locate and destroy Clarion's plague stores if possible, or at the very least secure the facilities they are housed in. This will allow us to send in teams of HAZMAT personnel who will then destroy the virus by fire."

She pinched the air and the screen zoomed in on North and South America, and after flicking her fingers upward and causing the planet to rotate south to north, she zoomed in on one of the red circles near the bottom of South America. She enhanced the image further, and it rushed outward to fill the four corners of the screen, revealing a complex of buildings on a dusty, mountainous plain.

"This is the base of operations in Tierra del Fuego, which is estimated to have 1,000 Clarion personnel at all times. Our comrades in the area will draw out the bulk of the defenders using a 500-person strong army regiment. This is expected to leave no more than 100 or so people in the base, and once the facility is so weakened, they will send in 10 agents to disrupt the facility's communications, electronic defenses, as well as blow up or at least disable as many of their physical weapons stores as possible."

A man at the right table raised his hand, and Nest called on him to speak.

He rose and Aveen saw that it was Huginn. "What is the expectation they would leave so important a base with such a diminished defense?"

Nest nodded as the man sat. "A good question. The reasoning is that if we were to attack with far greater numbers, they would simply stay inside. This facility is not truly a hardened one, but it offers greater protection against assault than fighting on open ground outside. But if they can see we are bringing less than half of their numbers to fight, they will be encouraged to emerge and crush us."

"Why not use agents to simply infiltrate the bases?" an older man at the left-side table asked.

"We cannot be sure of their ICE and antipersonnel defenses," Nest replied. "If we had more time we would do that very thing. But our intelligence tells us that Clarion is set to launch a massive, worldwide dispersal in less than a week. And after what you saw in the simulation, we can't take the risk of it getting out."

She zoomed out and rotated the globe until Romania and its familiar mountains and dense forests appeared. Three pulsing red dots showed on the screen.

"As to our own backyard, these are the bases in Romania we believe are manufacturing *entropy*. Radu, Buzdugan, and Matia are their names, and they are all slightly smaller than the Tierra del Fuego example I just provided. They are estimated to house approximately 75 full-time personnel. Most of these individuals are scientists and researchers, with a dedicated defensive force of only about 15 soldiers. Therefore," she said, zooming in on one to show a hardened facility made of enormous wedges of concrete set against the side of a cliff, "three four-person teams will be dispatched to secure them. They will be a combination of assault-equipped members and infiltration units. The teams are free to use any means that they feel are appropriate for the situation, be it immobilization rounds or other temporary restraints, up to and including all forms of lethal admission."

"But it has to be stressed," she added, turning to look out onto the faces looking back at her, "the purpose of this mission is to destroy their chemical weapons stores. The people of these facilities are secondary at best. Whether you meet stiff resistance or none, your goal is to locate the laboratories where the pathogen is housed and destroy them with incendiaries. If this is not possible, you must lock them down by any means until appropriate disposal technicians can do so. Once this is accomplished, you're instructed to take what prisoners you can, as well as retrieve any and all data from the facility's drives."

"Now then," she said, as half a dozen attendants entered the hall and began walking along the tables, "these are special Ramps you need to take in order to stave off the increased concentration of *dreamscape* out in the DOX. We haven't had the time to produce something which would protect you from *entropy*, but this will at least provide a basic defense against becoming Dreamers until you get to your targets. Everyone take a vial and administer it."

The attendants walked along the tables and Aveen and the others each took a thumb-sized plastic tube of faintly-glowing green liquid. He and his team considered the object in their hands, each looking to the other. They could not speak as openly as they had in the infirmary as they were surrounded by other agents. But it was clear that none of them felt right about taking the medication after what Dr. Jiang had said before dying in the Bucharest high rise.

Aveen saw that the rest of the table had cracked open and swallowed their Ramps, and he sighed as he raised his to eye level. "Well, I guess we'll have to have faith."

Benji gave him a look. "Huh. That doesn't sound like you. What happened to that whole 'the foolish believe, and then they die anyway' stance?"

"I didn't say faith in who gave us these," Aveen answered, before cracking his open and swallowing the dose. "I meant in each other."

He dropped the spent vial into the sharps box another attendant carried by and looked down at the floor, his mind on hidden tunnels and friends long vanished.

"And faith that Glider is still the man I remember," he murmured.

As the vials were passed out and collected, a member of the team opposite Aveen's leaned forward toward Celeste.

"Faith, huh? You guys have fallen to needing prayer for your runs? Why am I not surprised?"

Celeste turned from dropping her vial into the disposal box and met the woman's eye. "Oh, hey Ceelon. I didn't see you there. You really blend into the background."

Ceelon chuckled. "Yeah, that's me. I like to keep things quiet. That's why my girls will be leading the attack on Radu. You'll actually have competent leadership this time around, so you'll get to see my Valkyries get the job done without you bringing home another failure."

Celeste considered the woman's body armor and made a dismissive face. "You're a blunt instrument, Ceelon. A battering ram. And they always lead the charge. Then they get thrown aside to make room for the people who actually matter."

"The hotel where the Skip played you, the exams that nobody wants to talk about," Ceelon mused, not taken in by Celeste's bait. "And now you went and got the man you were sent to rescue killed. If it wasn't such pure incompetence, I'd think you were sabotaging yourselves."

"Oh, I'm sorry," Celeste said, giving her a puzzled and somewhat apologetic expression, "were you talking? I couldn't tell with you wrapped up in all that target practice armor. But hey, while you and Ladies Night stand around absorbing bullets, we'll be actually retrieving information and eradicating the virus. And don't worry," she added, as Ceelon looked at her with murderous eyes, "this will be your chance to make an impression. Who knows? You might even get to stop being a pillow biter for Clarion's rifles long enough to actually do something meaningful. Maybe you'll get to carry my Sack after

I download all the Clarion intel like I did on the last run. So chin up!"

Ceelon grinned, her calming expression suggesting far more beneath the surface than simple rage. "Real funny," she said, her eyes cold. "Just remember to take care out there. It's so easy to have accidents with live rounds and no witnesses. With my team running as heavies, you lightweights will be vulnerable to lucky shots. And I'd hate for something to happen to you when we're assaulting that base."

The guard called for attention again and Celeste looked away from the savage leer of the woman across from her. General Aepal strode onto the stage where Captain Nest saluted and withdrew. He looked out on the room and considered them as though weighing their worth. He nodded, satisfied with what he saw.

"Ladies and gentlemen, what is ahead of us will be difficult. But it is what you trained for nearly all of your lives. And now it is finally here: the chance to end the rebellion."

He placed his hands behind his back and began slowly walking along the front of the stage, the heads of those nearest to him tracking his passing. "The millions—billions—who died because of *dreamscape* can be accounted for," he said, "can be given rest. We can't bring them back, but we can bring those responsible for their deaths to book. We can stop them from finishing what they began 30 years ago. We are going into the lion's den and we're going to rip that beast's heart from its chest. And the world will heal. We will see the land return to ages past, before the Fence, before the plague."

He stopped walking and looked around the high walls of dusty brick and ribbed ceiling lost in the gloom above. "I'm sure some of you wondered why this room remained as it was. So many of you grew up here, spending time in smooth-walled rooms of sound dampening and kinetic energy absorbing. Modern and cutting edge. But here we are, in a room a thousand years past its prime. So out of date and out of place with the rest of the remodeled castle."

"When you think about it, the Protectorate is the same. It is a wedge of normalcy surrounded by a chaotic and troubled sea. Is that to say we should convert the planet into the past we sit in right now? No. That isn't what I mean. This castle was built in a time of war, by men and women who needed it to be hard stone and arrow slits. Once the war passed, rooms like this could be used for ceremonies and parties. Celebrations of life and the peace the earlier generations fought for."

He looked out over the faces, his own thoughtful and resolute. "We are coming to the same end of our war, my friends. We will go out and end the chaos and death that has blanketed the land for so many years. And when we do we will return to Corvin and see its combat centers and PSYOPs rooms, its firing ranges and ICE development labs, all changed to something better. We will come home and build the lives for ourselves we lost, alongside those we've given back. Over the next two to four days, we are going to change the world. Through sacrifice, we will change it to one of peace."

He let out a breath through his nose and began pacing again. "You all know our enemy and its capabilities. Each of you has proven their commitment to the just cause we are engaged in. But whatever training we have been able to provide you and the missions you have gone on, life in the DOX is something for which no one could really be ready.

"You will see a form of devastation we could not prepare you for. You will see natural beauty that hides horrific evil. You will see people seemingly immune to *dreamscape*, as well as those who feel like they could be your neighbors inside of the Fence. In short: you will come face to face with the unexpected, for which we cannot gird you." He looked up from where he had been considering the ground a few feet in front of him.

"But this is Clarion's trick; its greatest one. The landscape that is reclaiming so much hides their misguided and maleficent followers. Those individuals who seem like pitiful citizens or regular people who you might see walking down any one of our streets are very likely carriers for *dreamscape*, the symptoms not manifesting because of three decades' worth of slight changes that offer them some measure of protection. Houses and buildings that look perfectly livable might be the sites where families slaughtered each other, where dreams turned to nightmares."

He looked around at the hall as though seeing it for the first time. His eyes rested on a particular statue, or rolled along the ribs of the vaulted ceiling in slow, careful consideration. "When I first came to Corvin, it felt like a fairy tale castle to me. It seemed like something out of time; something that no longer belonged in the modern world. But there is a lesson in these surroundings," he added, bringing his gaze back down to his audience. "And it is the same one you take with you out into combat: the best of the past must support the building of a meaningful future. The men who built this place did so with a quality which supports us here ten centuries later. They were flawed, as we all are. Their views on gender and birthright are abominable to us today. And yet, their work shows who they really were. And yours, as you leave here to put an end to the greatest destructive experience of our species' history, shows who you really are."

He saluted the room and all snapped up to stand and return the gesture. He lowered his arm and walked off stage, as the room resumed its muted mumbling and pockets of conversation. As General Aepal stood for a minute talking to his senior aides,

Captain Nest approached and waited for him to finish. He did so, then turned to walk toward the door he had entered by.

"Captain. Something on your mind?"

Nest fell into step beside him as he walked along the eastern wall toward the back of the Great Hall. She waited until they had moved past the end of the tables and were a dozen paces from the agents who clustered around them.

She cleared her throat and spoke softly. "Yes, sir. I just wanted to note my concern with this operation."

His eyebrow raised slightly as they walked, but he did not look at her. "I see. And what is it which gives you pause?"

"The fact is, we're sending out our entire agent corps. Every Protectorate is. And a large chunk of our military and law enforcement personnel."

He nodded as they neared the door where a pair of guards stood on either side. "And you feel this leaves us vulnerable to a possible counterattack? All one's eggs in one's basket, so to speak?"

She eyed the guards and slowed her step so that they could not overhear her. "In essence. I understand the urgency and realize we couldn't trust Skips to this sort of mission. But it does seem extraordinarily risky to me."

Aepal nodded, taking in her words. "You are correct, Captain. It is an urgent operation, and one which might well see most of our people killed. But the alternative is too ghastly to allow. If our agents die in the process, so be it. If the units taking fire as a means of distracting the defenders from our people infiltrating are blown to pieces by artillery or gassed by shells filled with nerve agent, I have to accept it. So long as our agents get inside and retrieve or destroy the *entropy* stocks, it will be a victory. A pyrrhic one, it is true. But the stakes are too high to wait for a less costly one. If we hesitate, there may well be none of us left to even acknowledge our defeat. And the world will follow."

She saluted and he returned it, then stepped through the door to leave her standing there with a troubled expression.

17

SKY ASSAULT

*T*he assault into the DOX began before dawn broke in most of the areas surrounding the Protectorates, or just after sunset in the opposing hemisphere. It was coordinated to happen after their leaders dropped what they said were prototype bombs that dispersed a fine mist of nanites which would disrupt the communication arrays around the bases.

"It will prevent all communications going into and leaving the area," Captain Nest informed them, as the combined agent corps lined up for their respective transports. "So make sure the details of the target are well and truly committed before you jump. Once you're in the air, you're on your own. No comms, no extraction. You get in and get the job done, then hike out a dozen klicks and call for pickup."

This invisible tool would remain on the wind for 72 hours, spreading to cover a predicted one thousand square kilometers. The haze of electromagnetic pulses the nanites would give off would prevent Clarion from calling for reinforcements, and by the time anyone could spread the word of the assault, there would be no one left capable of doing so.

Radu turned out to be a ruined castle 70 kilometers east of Corvin, on the country's highest peak, Moldoveanu, in the Carpathian Mountains. The 12-person assault force consisting of Aveen's, Ceelon's, and another team flew quietly through the pre-dawn on black transports, which emptied them out 6,000 meters over the dark forest of Transylvania. Just before jumping into the night on their flight suits, Ceelon radioed to the combined force.

"All right, kids. This is it. We're dropping in to give those bastards a boot up the ass. Once we hit open air, we've got maybe a minute of radio before the nanite cloud cuts out our comms. So everyone stay together and make your way up the slope to the ruin upon landing. The LZ is a half-klick from the target, and it will be easy to spot from the air. It's the only open area in the forest besides the castle itself for ten kilometers. Make for it, regroup, and we head up."

She didn't ask if there were any questions, and none were raised. Two minutes later, everyone leapt from their respective trans-ports, which swung back in wide, lazy turns on their quiet, magnetic drives toward Corvin. Ceelon and her Valkyries took point, flying beneath the distant stars and above the wisps of cloud that traced the sky at two miles up. Once he was certain radio contact was impossible, Aveen flexed his arms and swung in a 180 degree turn back toward the west. His team, which had been at the rear of the formation, did likewise, and within thirty seconds they had vanished from sight, their black LT suits invis-ible against the dark forest, flying toward a different castle altogether.

Five minutes later, Ceelon landed in the clearing. She bounced a few steps due to the weight of her battle suit. But once settled, she turned and looked back at the dark sky, its gloom fading where dawn was showing the first touches of color from the east.

Her team landed shortly after she did, spacing themselves out so as not to collide. The second team did as well. They took a defensive position and stood with Scorpions raised in all directions as Ceelon kept her eyes on the skies. But Aveen's team was nowhere in sight.

"Goddamn it, where are they?" she hissed.

Thirty kilometers to the west, Aveen angled his shoulders and hips toward a thumb of rock that emerged from the thick forests overlooking the Argeş River. The land below him was dark with trees and the curving river that sliced through the valley between the low peaks of the Făgăraş Mountains was a long way below the small ridge of rock he was aiming for.

I miss that, I'm in the river. And it's a good 300 meters to fall.

Realizing if this were to happen, he wouldn't survive. He forced the image of crushing, watery death from his mind and focused on the landing. There was a flat area at the back of the ruin where earthquakes years earlier had felled the towers on that side, sending their stones crashing down to the river far below. In the dimness of almost dawn, he saw it was free of trees, and with no better place to aim for, he angled toward the open, mostly flat space.

He landed hard. His momentum carried him to the edge of the crumbling ruin, and he had to throw himself into a sideways slide to stop from sailing off the summit. The rest of his team landed with similar difficulties and the same results.

"Well! That was all kinds of fun," Benji said, snapping his hands and feet to his sides to draw the mesh of his wings into the seams of his suit. "But we made it. Now we can look forward to a court martial, a lovely stay in the PSYOP cells where they'll string cheese our brains, and finally send a pulse bolt through the skull to finish off the retirement package. I still can't believe I agreed to this," he added, his tone losing its cheery quality as his smile pulled inward like his suit's wings.

"Yes, we made it," Tofe said, pulling in his own membranes as Aveen and Celeste did likewise. "And Ceelon must've figured out we're not standing there with her in the clearing preparing to assault Radu. Fortunately, she cannot call back to Corvin to tell them we're AWOL."

"Regardless," Aveen said, scanning the stones of the ancient fortress in a search for a doorway or other portal, "we've made our play. It's what Glider would want us to do."

"Easy for him to say," Benji said, his Scorpion out and his own eyes crawling over the tan and faded red bricks of the nearby walls that hemmed them in. "He's dead. Speaking of what we're soon to be: Where is he in this godforsaken ruin?"

Celeste was thinking the same thing. She was about to tell Benji to quit whining and demand to know why he thought the ruins of the nation's cruelest leader was an ideal spot for the Protectorate's most decorated and disappeared agent, when the barrel of a gun pressed against the back of her head.

"You know, I always heard you guys were ghosts. You could appear and vanish at will, like the *bărbat zvelt.*"

A dozen barrels appeared, each poking out of a crack in the rock or from around the side of one of the stunted, twisted trees that grew from various points along stone walls. No one was visible, but the guns weren't holding themselves. Aveen raised his hands along with the rest.

The voice drew closer to her ear. "But I suppose one does have to outgrow fairy tales."

~

Thirty kilometers to the east, Ceelon had no choice but to go ahead with the assault.

As much as she hated Celeste, she didn't relish the idea of running up the slope with a third of her force unaccounted for. There was still a quarter of an hour before she had to commit to breaching the north side of the ruined citadel, according to the timetable ordered by General Aepal in conjunction with his nanite EMP, and she used it in an effort to search for the missing team.

"Jenkins!" she snapped, her eyes trained on the silhouette of the fortress 500 meters up the slope from her. "You find anything yet?"

"Negative," the woman replied after passing the message along by shouting into the dense forest. "We've tried thermals and sonics, and have got nothing to show for it. Wherever they are, they aren't here."

"Goddamn it," Ceelon murmured, her eyes straying to her watch. They had two minutes left before they assaulted the citadel, and she needed her people in position to make it happen. If she kept the eight members of her force in a rescue pattern, they would be out of position for an assault. And that could see them all killed.

Just as she was about to commit to sending in her reduced numbers to secure the base and take charge of the *entropy* stores, her second in command walked to her side.

"Ceelon, the radio is working."

She blinked. "That's impossible. The nanite cloud is supposed to—"

"I know what it's supposed to do," the woman cut across her, standing by the edge of the trees in her battle armor and pointing her left wrist back in the direction they came from. "But the radio's working. So you'd better ask for orders before we charge up the hill at two-thirds strength."

Ceelon frowned and made to rebuke her. But after a moment she clicked on her comm and nodded. "Son of a bitch," she said, her feeling of unease growing as she typed in the code for a secure line to Corvin.

Captain Nest sat in her office reviewing projections for the upcoming battles and wondering when she would actually receive reports from the ground, when the commlink on her desk flashed. She frowned and then reached for it.

"This is Nest."

"Captain! This is Radu team leader. We have a problem."

Nest leaned forward, her body tense with images of her people contorting and dying from exposure to the virus they were sent to destroy. "Team leader, what is your status?"

"We're in position at the base of the hill, and ready to assault. But one of the teams is missing."

Nest blinked. "Missing? They were captured?"

"No! They never arrived! It's Aveen's team."

Nest leapt from her desk and threw her hands up into the air. The screen she created by doing so was a blur of maps and reports, and she swiped them aside to leave a map of the Transylvanian forest. She zoomed in to show Radu Castle and the bare patch of ground Ceelon and her force was occupying. It wasn't a live satellite image, as the last one passed an hour earlier. But she quickly ran her eyes over the area looking for potential hazards that could have caused Aveen and his people to miss the landing zone.

Ceelon interrupted her examination with a request to either go ahead with the attack or withdraw. "Are you encountering any hostiles?" Nest asked, her eyes flying over the features of the map and seeing nothing that stood out as hazardous. There was another castle to the west, which her map indicated was called Poenari. It was conceivable Aveen had made for it instead of Radu. And with his comms out due to the nanite EMP, he wouldn't have been able to call for orders as Ceelon was doing.

But how the hell was she *doing it?*

Nest swore and turned back to the commlink on her desk. "Continue on with the mission. If you cannot secure the facility with your reduced squad, withdraw and monitor its activities. If anyone tries to leave to raise an alarm, detain them if possible. Kill if not."

"Understood. And Aveen's team?"

Nest sighed. "I tried raising them on the comm, but nothing so far. There is another castle a few klicks west of you, though. Once you've got Radu secured do a flyby to check if they dropped there by mistake. I'll have a transport standing by to take you."

Ceelon acknowledged the order and signed off. The other seven members of her team stood with weapons at the ready and grim looks on their faces.

"We're going in," she said, pulling her Scorpion around and selecting the highest level of lethal rounds. "Paulson, you and Keck blow the door once we're up the slope. The rest of us will cover you."

"What about Aveen?" Keck asked.

"Fuck him and fuck his incompetence," she snapped, the beginning of a headache pushing up from the back of her skull. "After we take this shithole we're going to another one to look for them. And he'd better hope we don't find them."

She motioned with her right hand for them to ascend the hill, and they moved out in a two-by-two cover formation with the explosives pair second from the front. She watched them jogging upward for a moment as she shook the stiffness from her hands. Then she ran after.

18

LIES BURIED

*A*veen and the others were disarmed and their hands tied behind their backs by the men and women who emerged from the rocks of Castle Poenari. This they actually did, and Tofe had to smile at the simple ingenuity of the site's defense.

"Holographic walls. Of course," he said, as the barrels pointed at them passed through the walls to be followed by grim-faced irregular soldiers in drab gray and black civilian clothing. "You don't need to post guards and build massive defensive structures if anyone flying by sees only what you want them to see."

The young man securing his bonds while two others pointed rifles at Tofe's head made a noncommittal sound. "We don't have the resources for giant earthworks and high-tech defenses. But then, having them doesn't ensure they can't be overcome by simple psychology. Dictators never think commoners can outwit them, although they're always afraid they'll beat them by force. So it wasn't hard to guess you Protectorate boys would rely on your advanced tech too much. It's in your name."

"Well, if you omit the 'h,' then yeah," Benji quipped, as his own guard shoved him toward the seemingly solid wall. He did not flinch as the dusty stones now lit by the rising sun pouring into the valley approached his face, and he stepped through the field imitating the ancient structure to find a staircase leading down a dark tunnel cut into the mountain. The others followed, and they were led down the roughly cut steps in a back-and-forth pattern to end at a steel grid platform with a door at one end.

The man who guarded Celeste stepped forward and rapped twice on the door, and a bolt slid back. It opened and Glider stood there smiling.

"'Journeys end in lovers meeting,' so the saying goes. But I doubt you're feeling all that happy to see me."

"Yeah," Aveen said, twisting with an angry jerk from the grip of his captor, "I'm feeling like I want to kick your ass."

Glider nodded, his expression accepting of the rebuke. "You should. But once you understand why I left, you'll forgive me." He nodded for them to enter, and as they passed by Celeste's guard paused. He let her go ahead and turned back to stand next to Glider.

"You're certain we can trust them? Aepal isn't above such deception as using friends and family to do his dirty work."

Glider watched them step into the large room where several screens and computer terminals glowed and beeped. He spoke softly to the guard. "You scanned them?"

"Of course. The usual implants you told us about, and their suits have GPS transponders built in. But the castle's field blocks them."

Glider nodded. "We'll need to disable them entirely. They'll be going outside."

The guard said nothing to this but frowned as he watched the four being led to a line of chairs and roughly shoved down onto them.

"Nothing biological?" Glider asked in a quiet voice.

The guard shook his head, looking back at his superior. "Nothing on the surface. You'd have to do a blood test to look deeper. You expecting something?"

Glider considered the four a dozen paces away. Aveen stared back at him with cold anger, Benji was still trying to chat with the people standing around him, Celeste looked troubled but was otherwise calm. Only Tofe looked around with an interested air, his expression thoughtful as his eyes traced the control room that had been constructed inside of a hollowed-out mountain.

Glider shook his head and closed the door, bolting it securely. "Keep their weapons and make sure there are always four guards on hand wherever they are. But you can free their hands. We need to make them see our side of the equation."

The guard's look was doubtful but not combative. "You really think they'll believe you?"

Glider gave a humorless laugh. "*Truth rises.* It's one thing the Protectorate got right. And they're here. That tells you they're open to what we have to show them."

"Unless it's a trick to get them inside and prove you're alive. And if they get into our network, they'll be able to find every other base across the planet."

"Hence why you're guarding them," Glider said, his tone taking on a warning note. "I didn't go to all of the trouble to get them out here just to hand over the keys to our defenses. If they come to our side, so be it. If not, they will be killed."

The guard sighed and nodded, not wanting to antagonize the man further. "Yeah. If what Guiterrez told us is true, we don't have much time. We need access to Corvin. If we don't get it from your old buddy," he added, nodding at Aveen, "we'll have to assault the place directly. And its defenses are more than just holograms."

Half an hour later saw them emerge from the base of the mountain through another holographic door, and Glider led them a ways beside the river to a large copse of trees. He walked into them and the others followed, his guests finding not a ruined outpost for the citadel above nor another high-tech control room carved from the rock of the valley, but a small village of a dozen structures.

The four looked around at the small huts and stone houses shaded by the massive trees, where a few dozen men, women, and children stared back. Glider lifted his hand and smiled.

"No worries, folks. They're friends."

This simple assertion melted the questioning looks from the people's faces, and they turned back to their conversations and activities.

Aveen walked beside Glider beneath the shade trees and murmured. "Friends. That's funny. You say that like it means something."

"I get it, you're pissed," he said, walking over to an old woman standing before a simple metal cart where the strong, rich smell of coffee emanated. He greeted her and half-turned back to Aveen to speak. "This is why I left. These people are who we were always meant to protect."

He bought five cups and thanked the woman selling them as he accepted his, and indicated for Aveen's team to take the others.

Aveen stared at the woman holding out a cup to him with tight lips. But he sighed and finally accepted it. Glider passed out three more to Celeste, Tofe, and Benji, then walked toward a ruined wall half a dozen paces away. Sections of its bricks were smashed by some long-ago battle, and the rock now bore winding strands of slender vines speckled with small white flowers, clutching it in their climb toward the same sunrise Glider looked up at with appreciative eyes. He gestured around.

"This place was devoid of people five years ago. That was the intention of General Aepal and the World Security Council. That goal hasn't changed."

"Why would they want to eliminate these people?" Celeste asked, coming to stand beside Aveen, and looking back at the tiny village. "They seem happy. No one's sick."

"And therein lies the greatest trick the devil ever pulled," Glider said, sipping his coffee.

He sighed. "You've always been taught that the globe was over-whelmed by *dreamscape*. The bubbles of magnetic energy that encircled the few uncorrupted cities acted as a barrier to any who would bring the infection inside and finish off the human race. But it's all a lie. It always was. And more than that, it wasn't Clarion that created the virus. The WSC leaned heavily into that narrative, which was natural. But we never created it. We did not even exist during the time of war prior to the plague."

"You keep saying 'we,'" Tofe said, watching Glider. "But you were an agent first. The most accomplished one, from what I've heard. How did you go from that to being in this terrorist group turned hot beverage enthusiasts? Or were you always a member, and joined the Protectorate as a plant?"

Glider grinned and shook his head. "No, I was a true believer. My family was decimated by the virus, and I wanted to hurt the people who had created it. I wanted to set things right after the horrors they let loose onto the world during the Plague War."

"What changed you?" Aveen asked, his expression slightly less tense.

Glider looked back at the coffee cart and the small village nestled in the trees. Children played, running around and shrieking beneath the dappled light of the sun shining down through the leaves. Old people sat on chairs or stools and talked as though they weren't living in a toxic wasteland crawling with infected Dreamers. He sighed with a small, regretful smile.

"They did. Not them specifically, but those like them. The regular people of the world I was supposed to be protecting. I was sent out on a mission to evaluate the DOX in a twenty-klick section for its concentration of Dreamers, and to destroy the ones I came across as you might swat mosquitos. I thought it was right, and I set out with extra clips and an eagerness to cut a swath through the infected which had robbed me of my family."

He sipped his coffee and looked down along the river shining with the morning. "But what I found were other families. Other kids fighting to hold onto their own little patch of the world, with parents who were doing the same as they tried to keep their children and themselves from turning into walking nightmares. I found places like this."

He looked into his cup. "I killed a lot of people before I woke up. Because it was *me* who was dreaming. I was when I met you," he said, looking to Aveen. "I was a scared, angry kid trying to be cool. Trying to change a world he thought he understood. But when I came out here to scout for the infected and put them all down, I found echos of what I lost. And after I had killed some of them believing them to be infected, I was faced with the reality I was the virus. I was the one ending lives that might have been saved."

Aveen sat there and said nothing for a while, holding his cup in both hands and staring into its depths. Finally he took his first sip and cleared his throat.

"You taught me to always find a flaw. To look for the weak spot and exploit it. How do I know they didn't do it with you? That someone figured out your dead family was your trigger to stop you from pulling the one on your rifle?"

Glider nodded. "Yeah, that's fair. And you're right; PSYOPs taught me to expect such strategies from the enemy. The *mencists* hammered home the idea that the plaguers profiting from selling their garbage cures would do everything they could to stop me from slicing through their customer base."

"So what did?"

"The truth. Just like Aepal always says: it rises. And he would know, having buried so much of it over the years."

He explained how he had been out in the DOX for several weeks and was set to return to report at Corvin in two days' time, his doubts about the prevalence of the virus beginning to bother him, when he witnessed a Protectorate team setting up something at night outside of one of the tiny villages Glider had determined housed no infected people.

"They set up gas bombs on the windward side, so that the breeze would blow it through the old stone houses and pitiful shelters most were living in. I watched them time the charges to blow an hour later, giving them plenty of time to get clear of the initial dispersal and any blowback a change in the wind would cause. This gave me the chance to examine the ordinance five minutes after they cleared out, and when I figured it was some kind of chemical bomb about to wash over a sleeping village of innocent civilians, I disarmed all of them. And before I left the village and returned to Corvin, I buried all of the canisters."

Aveen considered him. "That was a call you shouldn't have made. They had their orders, and if the command didn't share them with you, so be it. What right did you have to undercut those soldiers' efforts?"

"The right to life!" Glider snapped, anger flaring in his face. "They didn't even try to evaluate the place! They just snuck in during the middle of the night and set up chemical bombs! The Second Geneva Convention might have allowed for 'extraordinary measures to contain the virus', but they also called for specific protocols to be observed before doing so. Things like sending in surveyors on the ground to determine if we had to burn the village to save it."

"People like you," Benji said, speaking without humor for the first time.

Glider turned to him, his anger ebbing. "Yes, people like me. I lost my family to an incendiary bomb when I was ten, and always blamed Clarion for it. Or at least the 'terrorists' who would become them," he added, sending a look at Tofe. "But that night was the first time I saw Protectorate forces carrying out the same indiscriminate murder as had killed mine and so many other families. It was the first time I considered that both sides were guilty, and more than that, perhaps one had been hurting the innocent under the guise of protection all along."

Celeste swallowed at this but said nothing. In her mind, she saw her final exam to become an agent, and the man before them warning her not to hurt the wrong people. And she had. That very night, she had.

As they began talking about how Glider made his way back to Corvin and turned in an honest account of his findings (omitting sabotaging the clandestine chemical attack), she slowly sat on the wall. The man she had killed came back to her. He, and his partner. Both men were kind, she recalled. Both were full of the contentment lives well spent and deeds done for the right reasons provided. She could feel the quiet satisfaction they had in themselves and each other as she dropped a poison pill into their drinks after a distraction pulled their attention away.

I watched them die. I watched them tremble and clutch their stomachs as the toxin wormed its way through them. I watched them clutch at each other and cry out for help that wouldn't come. That wouldn't have saved them. And yet I called for it myself. I cried out for someone to do something. To undo what I had done.

A tear slid down her cheek to fall into her cup. It sent out ripples that rebounded against the sides of the glass, and she felt sick inside. The sun and the sound of children's laughter was all around her, and she felt nothing but cold, heavy guilt. As Glider had warned her at the bar before she went over to snuff out a pair of lives, the Protectorate was hurting people. And as he had said, she was one of them.

She set the cup on the stones beside her and a curl of vine with several white flowers looped around the drink in reaction to her placing it against the green. She watched the plant gently embrace the cup, her soul yearning to get away, to run as Glider had done years before. But there was nowhere for her to go where the dead wouldn't follow her. And she couldn't ask the others how they were feeling about killing their targets. None of them were wrestling with the horror of what they had done as she was. She could see it on their faces as they listened to Glider explain how he had found peace and new purpose under the therapeutic mentoring of Elena, an old *mencist* on staff at Corvin.

Only two of their class had failed to execute their targets that night a month earlier, and General Aepal himself had seen to their expulsion.

"So you and this Elena left Corvin on the pretext of another reconnaissance run into the DOX?" Tofe asked, and Glider nodded.

"There was nothing left for me there. Except the people I had come to trust and rely on," he nodded at Aveen, "and they couldn't come with me. One man can only make one man's difference, and I wanted more. I wanted to be a part of something greater, to take the place of the false one I had been tricked into serving. Elena knew of the resistance and had made secret contact with some of them. So we left to join them, and afterward Aepal told yet another lie in saying we had died out in the DOX."

"You keep saying 'trick,'" Aveen said, his voice tight with conflicted anger and doubt. "But the Protectorate provides food and medical care, education and safe places to live! And you're saying it's all a lie, that everything we've been doing was just supporting murder and genocide!"

Glider let the anger pour without trying to stop it. Aveen was clutching at the last desperate hope the man before him was wrong. That Glider had run away when he should have stayed, that he was just wrong about what he had seen and done. Because if he was right, he did what Aveen should have done. He left before he could damn himself further, in the way his former mentee had.

Glider rose from the wall and motioned for them to walk back toward the hidden doorway at the base of the cliff the ruined castle perched on. "The Protectorate does as you say. It gives its citizens all they need to survive and even prosper. But it is all built on a lie. And one you would never support if you knew what it was. And when I tell you what that deception is, you will see all of the education and health care it provides is little more than flakes of food dropped for an ignorant group of captive goldfish."

They reached the base of the cliff and the holographic door, and Aveen reached out and jerked Glider back to face him. The guards all snapped their rifles up to point at Aveen's head, but Glider raised his hands and motioned them down.

Aveen ignored the weapons and got right in Glider's face. "What makes you think that any of this is going to change our minds? That we're going to abandon our friends like you did and come squat out here in the waste? Why should we believe any of this?"

Glider met his gaze without flinching. "If I was just one man, trying to make a difference, I wouldn't believe me either. But in the decade I've been away, I've seen things and met people. I've seen the greater cause from the inside, and it's not just about a little boy looking to hurt someone because he lost his family. And you need to wake up and see that, Aveen. This isn't about you or me, or being on the winning side. It's about the greatest lie the Protectorate ever told."

"What lie?" Celeste asked, stepping closer.

Glider looked at her. "Those canisters set up outside the village that night weren't just some nerve agent to get rid of a pocket of the infection in the DOX." He looked back and locked eyes with Aveen. "It was *dreamscape* itself. And it wasn't the first time they gassed innocent people. They've been doing it ever since I left. And right now you're helping them carry out the biggest mass murder in the history of the planet, under the guise of stopping *us* from dispersing a weapon far worse than the one they released 30 years ago."

He turned to walk toward the holographic portal and Tofe called out: "You're trying to tell us that *we're* helping plant these canisters to gas people? That's insane! We're not carrying anything like that!"

Glider paused and turned his head back to look downward. "Not in your hands, it's true. But you are carrying it within you. Your own leadership sent you as fireships to set the world outside the Fences ablaze."

19

TRUTH RISES

*C*aptain Nest leaned back in her chair and rubbed her eyes. She didn't know what to believe. Operation Northwoods was going according to plan, as far as she could tell. Which in and of itself was worrying. She shouldn't have to go on *feeling*. She should have dozens of files open in the air before her desk, each showing maps of troop movements, weather reports, casualty lists, and so forth. Even the news was off, due to the World Security Council's edict calling for a 48-hour moratorium on all broadcasts and Interlink services.

But with the communications blackout, that is what she had left. The smattering of reports she had been able to piece and patch together came from inadvertent messages by persons such as Ceelon, and even those ceased not long after she commed in to say Aveen's team was missing. The rivalry between her and Celeste was well-known, and Nest's initial reaction was to think Ceelon was making the call to cast shade on her counterpart.

But their GPS units were not working, and they hadn't tried to call in. Nest's attempts to raise them on their comms likewise went nowhere, but she shouldn't have been able to reach them.

The whole purpose of the blackout had been to prevent Clarion from coordinating a counterattack, and in this it was successful. The entire communication system was down, leaving Nest to feel a kindred sympathy for the military leaders of the past. From Julius Caesar to Napoleon, the generals had to rely on the speed of pen on paper for updates on their operations. And she didn't even have that; she couldn't have found a piece of paper and a pen in Castle Corvin if she searched for a year.

And here she was surrounded by technical capacity those leaders could never have dreamed of, and yet she had less knowledge of her own people than they. Ceelon's state as well as those of the other agents assaulting bases across Romania, she had no idea. Aveen's fate and his people, she knew less than nothing. She didn't have the people to send for a rescue mission, and even if she had, she didn't know where to direct them.

In her opinion, Operation Northwoods should never have been approved, much less carried out. It was illogical and even foolhardy to commit the WSC's entire agent corps to a single mission. The inability of the Clarion bases to take advantage of this and assault the Fences, as they could not combine their forces to do so while Protectorate ones were doing that very thing to their strongholds, meant the risk to the cities was minimal. But it was still something that should have been planned out over more time than the 48 hours the WSC had granted. Such a monumental task required a considerable amount of planning.

Nest rose and stalked to the half dozen floating files she had managed to acquire. The first was a satellite image of the Western Sahara where a force of 200 soldiers and police worked alongside two dozen of North Africa's top agents. Their assault on the remote fortress of Tassili n'Ajjer saw a series of images Nest examined minutely. The first showed the tawny sandstone of the desert from several thousand feet in pre-dawn light, which gave her the view of the distant low hills and dry riverbeds surrounding the ancient outpost. Subsequent images zoomed in and showed the attack force making its way toward the ancient walls first erected during the Carthaginian occupation. The people of Tyre were eventually driven off, but their fortress remained. Now it was occupied by a crack collection of hardened veterans in addition to the scientists cooking up their second wave of plague.

Nest peered in at the third of four images which showed the dark dots of people in a two-by-two approach pattern. These were the agents, and to the north on the other side of the citadel was the much larger group of soldiers and police meant to draw the attention of the defenders.

The last photo taken before the satellite orbited out of range showed the agents penetrating the southern side of the complex and the defenders focusing their fire on the north. She had no further images to consider, so she could not know how successful—or badly—the operation had gone for the North African teams. She had to assume it went all right. What else could she do but hope? And that its success reflected the globally-coordinated mission.

Globally coordinated, she sighed, as she looked at the other scraps of information she had been able to gather. The charts, the reports, the *socialink* postings from the odd civilian who had witnessed an operation happening within sight of their city.

God, it should never have been approved!

She would never have said this to General Aepal. Just bringing up her mild concern over the idea of coordinating a planet-wide assault on four dozen targets following his speech in the Great Hall to Corvin's entire Agent corps was an act of bravery on her part. She wasn't afraid of the general. She had too much respect for him. He was a father to her in many ways, itself another statement she would never make to him.

Turning from the smattering of largely unhelpful intelligence documents, she returned to her desk and sought to focus on what she could control. The disappearance of Aveen's team was the primary area of concern. She reached across the desk and swiped at the air in front of it to close the files. This done, she pulled up the fitness reports of Aveen and each of his members, as well as the records of their last missions. The syncs were of special interest, as they showed what the team was facing in real-time without filter or prejudice.

She made a habit of personally reviewing each team's syncs after their assignments for feedback and intelligence-gathering purposes. She hadn't done this on the Dr. Guozhi rescue mission as the sudden urgency of the data they had brought back from it had made such concerns irrelevant. A catastrophic viral release that would paint the world in new red had pushed aside all normal proceedings, and she hadn't thought to go back and examine the files.

She had visited them in the infirmary to check on the status of their quarantine and thought they seemed more tense and thoughtful than usual. At the time she had dismissed it as how anyone would act when waiting to hear from a doctor about whether they would be fine or would die a slow and painful death, their minds shredded as they descended deeper into the madness of *dreamscape*. It never occurred to her to probe deeper.

Twenty minutes later she was about to close all of their files and go to General Aepal's office to report their disappearance, when one of the syncs caught her attention.

"Wait ... what was that?"

She leaned forward onto her desk and reached out to pinch the air. This stopped the recording the agent's lenses made when he initiated it. She had already seen the other sync, in which the patrol marching along the street paused outside the building when Benji had trouble with his landing on the roof above. This recording was different, showing the interior of the target's apartment where three of the team were each covering a scientist, and Nest squinted at the scene that had given her pause.

Dr. Guozhi stood looking straight at her with coldness, and she knew it was directed at his rescuer. The man seemed about to say something when suddenly a shriek sounded on Benji's left. He spun to see an old woman in a white lab coat rise up from the other side of an overturned metal table and begin firing. The agent covering her shot back and the old woman was struck with a dozen Bulldogs in the torso. This lifted her off her feet and threw her back to slam into the wall, and as she fell Benji's eyes turned back to Dr. Guozhi. The old man clutched his neck with a look of pained surprise as blood leaked through his fingers and sank to the floor. The sync stopped as other shots rang out and the air before her desk changed to static.

The report Aveen turned in described this exact sequence of events, but something had caught her eye. She did not know what it was, but something about the way Dr. Guozhi was standing when Benji looked to the left at the old woman and her gun struck Nest as off. She rewound the last ten seconds of the sync and went through them frame by frame. Then she had it: the old man was suddenly looking directly at Benji's eyes when the next frame showed him looking down and to the left. Of course, a person could make the movement with their head or even just their eyes. But it was not instantaneous; a transition happened as the gaze changed from one point of focus to the next. And this one lacked it. The old man was looking at her with cold dismissal, and then simply staring somewhere else.

It was a small thing, but it was enough. Nest found other inconsistencies in the recording at the same instant the figure's gaze jumped impossibly. Where his shoulders were, the curve of his chin, the light on the side of his nose. Someone had doctored the sync, and who had done it and why would take time to uncover. But the reason for it was obvious: something happened during the operation that either Benji or one of his team wanted to remain buried.

She immediately applied the full suite of decryption programs and electronic scrubbers she had to the file, and within five minutes, a combination of brute force attacks and careful tweaks to the code showed her the entire sync, undoctored and clear.

And horrifying.

She rewound the recording to where Dr. Guozhi—no, not Guozhi but Jiang, a man supposed to have died years earlier—claimed Clarion wasn't developing an upgraded *dreamscape* pathogen but had found the cure to the original.

"But how is this possible?" she called out to the room, angrily shoving her chair back from the desk as far as the hovering magnetic seat would allow. "How in God's name could the general not find the cure in the files they brought back?"

For a moment the idea flashed through her mind that Aveen and his team were traitors, who had worked to keep the truth from Aepal in order to keep the war alive. Because if the cure for *dreamscape* was found, so much of the hostilities between the two sides would have to cease. The war would be nonsensical; everyone would be on the same side.

Of course, if there was a new virus, it would make peace impossible. It would make Operation Northwoods necessary.

But the notion a group of twenty-something agents who had no blemishes on their reports would somehow concoct a scheme to drive the World Security Council to demand a blitzkrieg on the Clarion outposts where chemical weapons were potentially capable was even more nonsensical. And even were such an insane scheme possible, what was the motive? Money made no sense, nor did any kind of advancement—political, military, or otherwise. It simply didn't compute that Aveen and his team would have been behind it.

And yet they concealed the sync's recording.

Nest shook her head, a headache forming in the back and pressing forward. She had uncovered something shocking that could well see the old negotiations between Protectorate and Clarion leadership return to the table for peace talks. But she had also found questions of loyalty and motive that did not answer so easily. Why had Aveen's team concealed what Dr. Jiang had said? Where were they, and what did they hope to accomplish with their disappearance?

Nest rubbed her eyes and felt exhausted. Ever since the directive from the WSC had come down for Operation Northwoods, she had not slept well. And the revelation, however troubling and far from complete, of Aveen's people hiding something so important, promised to steal other hours of her rest in the coming days.

She had just stood and removed a drive containing the unscrubbed mission that saw Dr. Jiang die with the intention of taking it to General Aepal, when her comm beeped. She leapt forward and hit the button on her desk for the call to come through.

"Yes? This is Nest. Report!"

A heavy sigh of pain and obvious weariness filled the comm. "Captain? This is Ceelon."

"Ceelon?" Nest asked, surprised. "What is happening? Where are you?"

A drunken-sounding giggle filled the room. "Where you told me to go. I found the castle where Celeste ran. Ran like a bitch!"

Nest frowned. "What are you talking about, Agent? You found Aveen's team?"

"Yeah, I did," the response came at once, full of anger and resentment. "We got into Radu, and killed everyone. Nobody's there now. And you know what? They tried to give us *entropy*. Said it was the cure. The fucking cure for *dreamscape*. The—the," she paused, her words slurring, "the fix for it all. Tried to give it. Tried to offer it. But we stopped 'em. Stopped 'em dead," she finished, as the comm filled with a sigh.

Nest cleared her throat, the idea Ceelon had just destroyed untold doses of the cure twisting her guts. But she forced herself to speak softly and simply. "Agent, you did find stocks of something? Which they said was the cure for *dreamscape*? You're certain the base wasn't preparing to disperse a chemical plague?"

Ceelon giggled. "Plague? Shit, I don't know. They had a lot of stuff, but we torched it all. Sent it all up in flames, baby!"

Nest closed her eyes and tried to keep her voice even, what she was hearing connecting with what she had just uncovered on the doctored sync making her heart race. "Okay. You clearly have encountered something that altered your consciousness. That's all right. Don't worry about it. But you say you're where I sent you? Where is that?"

"Bitch! Don't you remember?" Ceelon spat, making Nest grit her teeth at the insubordination. "You said the castle to the west! We're here. We're ready to fuck them up."

"We? Who is there?"

"My Valkyries, that's who," Ceelon said with something like pride, as her words trailed off. "The others? Yeah, they didn't want to come."

Nest felt something drop in her stomach. "The other team? They're still at Radu?"

Ceelon sounded like an angry drunk when she finally answered. "Stupid guys. Always screwing things up … "

"Agent, where is the other team?"

A pause, and her voice was less certain. "Had to kill 'em. Tried to kill us first … "

Nest's world was unraveling as she listened to the unhinged Agent. "Ceelon, listen to me. You were exposed to something. I don't know what it was, but it's obvious something infected you. Did a hostile spray you with something?"

Ceelon snorted, and the sound of women yelling something nearby with several shots and screams cut short sounded over it.

"Pfft! Nothing. We didn't let nothing come near us. Just flew through the cloud of nanites an' touched down. The cloud we put down, the Protectorate put down for us…" she trailed off as though distracted or not able to focus. Then she returned to the topic, her voice increasingly slurred. "Yeah, the nanites. Keep Clarion from dialing out. That was there. And after we shot everyone in Rad-rad something...

"Radu?"

"Yeah. We shot the fuckers and grabbed the transport west. And now we're in this valley. Got hills on both sides. And a castle up on a cliff. Celeste's there, right?"

Nest swallowed. Her three-team force was down by two-thirds, the first from a disappearance she couldn't explain, and the second portion apparently killed in a firefight with Ceelon's group. It was a nightmare any way she looked at it. And if Aveen's team was inexplicably inside Poenari, they were about to be shot by a group of psychotic teammates.

And I need them alive to explain what the hell happened in Bucharest, and hopefully salvage some of this clusterfuck of a mission.

"Agent, I want you to stand down," Nest finally said. "I appreciate the tremendous job you and the other agents have done, but we need to take an accurate assessment of the situation. And Aveen and his people might be under guard. We don't know what caused them to veer off course, and we have to ensure their safety."

"Safety!" Ceelon yelled, the sound filling Nest's office like a reverberating bomb. "Bitch went rogue! Only one way to deal with that. Gotta put her down. Gotta put 'em all down."

Nest started to tell her to stop, that she had to come back to base and not to assault the place where Aveen's team might be, when Ceelon cut the call off. Nest tried to raise her on the comm, but there was no answer.

Made in the USA
Las Vegas, NV
01 October 2021